Seven Sisters

By

M.L. Bullock

Dedication

This book is dedicated to my best friend and sister Karena. Thank you for endless summer days on bicycles, for sharing your blanket and keeping our room tidy. You are the best non-speaking actress I have ever met.

"Many a night I saw the Pleiades

Rising thro' the mellow shade

Glitter like a swarm of fire-flies

Tangled in a single braid."

Alfred Lord Tennyson

"Locksley Hall"

1842

Prologue

Mobile, AL, 1850

Her white hand shone like bone in the moonlight. Shivering, she stood perched on the walkway that led to the Delta Queen. To the casual observer, she might appear to be a statue, standing perfectly still, leaning slightly against the shiny wood railing. No, she was not a cold, unmoving statue but a real woman alive and free for the first time.

Musical notes jostled with one another in the air, and the voices of spirited patrons rolled from the riverboat like waves lapping along the shores of the Mobile River. Above the glittering riverboat hung a clear, dark sky filled with heavy stars that shone with an unusual brilliance. She heard no familiar voice but to her, those stars, the Pleiades, shone their approval like a message from heaven. Her lips turned up in a small smile as she imagined her mother saying, "Run—be free. Be what I can never be!"

She raised her hand to her lips to calm her heart—it leapt like a calf! She turned her head slightly, her long curls brushing her bare back. Looking down the sandy, moonlit path, she gave a small wave and smiled into the darkness at the friend she left behind. Then she disappeared into the bubbling soiree aboard Mobile's most celebrated ship.

Once inside, the young woman was thankful for the music. She was sure that without it, all of Mobile would hear the pounding of her heart. Clutched at her side was a small satin purse, elegantly beaded and embellished with silk ribbons. She slid her hand into the purse and pulled out a small, leather-bound book, running a finger over the cover. The book had changed her forever. Inside were his words, which had opened her closed heart. Like Ali Baba whispering the words that had opened the enchanted door.

How beautiful and courtly were his words! How completely he had allayed her every fear. She had carefully gathered each letter and bound them in her book. They had given her the courage to forget the darkness that had surrounded her.

Suddenly, anxiety overwhelmed her. What if he no longer wanted her? What if she had been too late in her reply? Would she now pay for her aloofness? She could never go back! She had done the unthinkable. The die was cast.

Somewhere aboard the Delta Queen was Captain David Garrett, the gentleman who had liberated her heart. The riverboat would leave Mobile soon. She had seized her chance, a chance at happiness away from the ghosts of Seven Sisters. She would reveal her soul to him, the man who had proven worthy of her love and devotion. His writings had plucked at her courage, creating a crescendo of hope, love and desire that commanded release. It would be fulfilled by her spontaneous act of affection—her willingness to leave behind a world of favor and prominence for a more uncertain one as his bride.

She moved through the thick wooden doorway, humming along to the waltz that flowed out of the concert hall. A woman with vulgar red lips smiled up at a mustached man who held two glasses overflowing with some sort of dark libation. Callie's disgust shook her back to her task. She hated hard drink; it made good men evil.

Her green eyes glittered as she searched the hall for Captain Garrett's dark, handsome countenance. She had seen him less than a dozen times, but she had sketched his face perfectly in her mind and added details after each visit, like the curl of his hair and the dark fringe of his eyelashes. Always his hair curled around his crisp white collars. His wide, toothy smile and cleft chin made him look like an exotic Russian prince, she imagined. She would recognize those dark blue eyes in a crowd of a hundred men.

She moved amongst the partiers, touched and jostled by dancers and couples flirting. Such a different world from the ballrooms of the local plantations where elegant ladies prided themselves on navigating the crowd without crushing another debutante's dress! A few gentlemen tipped their hats to her, but she was largely ignored. Her coral-colored silk gown, his favorite, rustled as she continued her quest.

Again, those questions screamed like banshees in her mind. What if he no longer wanted her? What if she had been too late in her reply?

She could never go back to her unhappy life. The dark thing she had witnessed, the many dark things she had seen, made that impossible. Her desperation rising, she asked a short, officious-looking man where the captain was. He silently led her through a myriad of hallways with a slow gait that irritated her. He tossed her a curious look once over his shoulder, and then unceremoniously left her standing in the hall outside a wooden door with a bronze handle.

She fussed over her barrette and pinched her cheeks for some color, as her mother had taught her to do. She was no hothouse rose like her cousin, but the flush of warmth in her cheeks flattered her thin nose and unusually full lips. It gave her an added sense of attractiveness. She felt confident, beautiful and wanted by this man of honor and gentility.

She raised her hand to knock, but then changed her mind. Instead, she followed her inner streak of boldness, the same boldness that had led her to this place, to this moment. Smiling to herself, she swung open the door. "David," she called out softly, laughing joyfully at saying his name aloud for the first time. The intimacy thrilled her.

No answer came. She stood silent in the small parlor, embarrassed but determined to find him.

Soft moans and a shimmer of light filtered through an open door. She strained to hear the hushed voices. Frozen momentarily in the shifting light of flickering candlelight and a rising moon, her heart raced to keep up with what her mind already knew.

"David, David! Oh, yes!"

As quietly as possible, she delicately pushed the door open wider. Standing perfectly still, she said nothing. She did nothing. The forgotten book slipped from her hand, making an odd slapping sound as the leather cover hit a space of bare wooden floor.

Half-dressed, his body exposed, his normally perfect coiffure of dark curls unruly and wild, David Garrett stood to face her. Even in the dim light, she could see his blue eyes. How easily they reflected his emotions—a flicker of realization, regret, and then sadness. Had he ever truly loved her? He opened his mouth to offer her his words, a reproach, perhaps an explanation. But she raised her hand in protest, surprising him into silence for a seemingly eternal moment.

From behind him there was a shuffling of clothes, then a familiar face peeking around his legs, a round cherubic face. Callie's cousin rose from the small, rumpled bed and stood standing next to the half-dressed captain. Her skin gleamed with sweat, evidence of her extreme betrayal. A blue gown lay piled on the floor, one that Callie recognized as her own. The half-naked girl giggled again, wrapping herself around David. Then she stretched out her hand to Callie, as if inviting her to join them. The scandalous move seemed to bring the captain to his senses; he scolded her loudly for her vulgar gesture and tried to dress himself as graciously as he could with a sense of obvious urgency.

Lifting her skirts with one hand and pushing him away with the other, Callie ran from the room, leaving the muskiness of the betrayers' lovemaking and her childish dreams behind. She ran blindly down the long hallway, through the unfamiliar complex of passageways that were now filled almost to capacity. She made her way through the crowd, running when she could.

She was thankful for the tears that blurred her vision. She didn't want to see the faces, the witnesses to her great shame. She welcomed the deepening agony, the hurt of the betrayal, the overwhelming sadness. Behind her she heard someone call her name. She never looked back.

Before she understood what was happening, she felt herself falling, falling into the blackness of the river. Above her, his outstretched arms, a quiet scream, silver stars, welcoming warmth, and then—nothing.

Chapter 1

I climbed into my blue Honda, slipped it into neutral and slid silently down the driveway. I hated saying goodbye to the comfortable garage apartment that smelled like fresh paint and new wood; however, I felt an unusual call to leave for once. I had the courage to go. That Zen-like, "I'm starting over" spell comforted me on this unseasonably cool morning as I slid the last box of my belongings into the backseat of the car. The rest, a collection of CDs, memorabilia from a recent trip to the Bahamas and most anything that did not fall into the jeans and t-shirt category, I left behind in a small storage space about a mile away. I had paid for six months in advance but was already putting off the idea of coming back to Charleston.

I did feel a twinge of guilt as I put the car into gear. I had not even bothered to say goodbye to William, my friend and sort-of boyfriend. He was kind and good and understanding, but I knew that would never last. We were too different in too many ways to describe. Perversely, I liked leaving on a high note, without the nightmares and all the screaming. It felt like a personal triumph. I was being selfish, but I was okay with that. At least for the moment.

"Once I make up my mind, the die is cast," I said to no one in particular.

I muttered, "Well, if I am stubborn, I have had to be." I already loathed myself for traveling down this predictable mental highway, but what else could I do for the next few hours but drive and think? I hadn't "gone there" in a while, so perhaps a quick review would be healthy. I rolled my eyes at myself in the rearview mirror. I sounded just like my last shrink. "How can I help you if you won't share with me, Carrie Jo? Why won't you let someone in?" Feeling a softness that I rarely experienced, I had pulled back the cover and let the light hit my secret for the first time in a long time.

* * *

"I'm not trying to be difficult, but without significant personal discipline, I would have gone nuts—like my mother, a long time ago." Encouraged by the petite, smiling psychologist, perched in her overlarge leather chair, I continued on, "You see, Dr. O'Neal, I have a problem—I dream about the past. I'm kind of like a human DVR; my dream life is usually not my own. It belongs to whatever memory movie plays the loudest wherever I'm sleeping."

Dr. O'Neal had looked at me blankly, unshaken by my confession.

Okay, the young, pretty doctor has earned ten points for the poker face she's wearing, I'd thought wryly. Her focused attention encouraged me to ramble on.

"That's why I love my garage apartment so much. It is brand spanking new, with no movies, no memories. I sleep, and I dream my own dreams. My 'problem' gets even more complicated when I sleep with someone else. I can see their dreams too."

Luckily, there haven't been too many of them, I'd thought, but I hadn't felt the need to share my lack of a love life with the dainty Dr. O'Neal, new bride and smart career woman. Her fingers had flown across her notebook, her manicured hands busy recording her undoubtedly smart thoughts to form a brilliant pre-diagnosis. I'd discreetly peeked at the wedding photo perched on her mahogany desk. It didn't take a degree to see she was proud of her groom.

I hated the silent moments of this confession, so I blathered on, in a hurry to make my point and come to the reason for my visit. That was me: give it to me in black and white, and I'll do the same for you.

"You see, Dr. O'Neal, I have this great job offer—it's a once-in-a-lifetime gig, really. But I hate giving up my apartment. I just don't know what to expect. That's why my friend Mia suggested I come see you. And, well, here I am."

To her credit, the shrink didn't zero in on my "problem"; instead, she took a sidestep that I hadn't anticipated. "What about your current relationships? Didn't you say you were seeing someone?" Consulting her notebook, she pointed. "Yes, he's a 'fantastic' guy. Don't you find it odd that you're worried about leaving your safe apartment but not this 'fantastic' guy?"

I left her office feeling deflated, insecure and even more confused. Why had I mentioned William? Obviously, Dr. Happily Married was going to focus on the sex angle rather than the real problem. When she called a few days later to setup a dream clinic session, it was a moot point. I had already made up my mind. I was leaving, come hell or high water. I had to take a chance away from the safety and security of my little apartment. I had to go where the work was. And although I couldn't explain it, even to myself, I knew my destiny waited for me in Mobile.

* * *

As I zipped onto the highway and left Charleston behind me, a ball of anxiety settled in the pit of my stomach. What was I doing traveling into the unknown? What night terrors would I experience in Mobile? I had to admit this kind of bold, brash move was surprising, even for me. Still, like the proverbial moth to a flame, I drove down the slick highway, drowning out the voice of Cautious Carrie Jo with the hum of my old faithful car. I smiled at myself in the rearview mirror as a sort of encouragement.

Behind my oversize sunglasses was a pair of almond-shaped green eyes. I liked my eyes; they reminded me of my father. At least that's what I figured, since they weren't anything like my mother's. I had never met my father. That morning, I had quickly piled my mass of brown, curly hair on top of my head in a messy ponytail bun. A few brown strands whipped around my face like wildcats in the wind as I sang along with Natalie Merchant. I dug in my purse for my favorite coral-colored lipstick. The shade looked pretty and bright against my light olive skin. I smiled at myself again to make sure the lipstick hadn't smeared on my teeth. I rarely wore lipstick, but somehow I felt like I needed to today. I felt free and happy.

"Funny how I got here," I pondered absently, glad to let the mental review of my conversation with Dr. O'Neal fade away. A few letters, a polished phone call from an attorney. It seemed like something I had read or dreamed about, but everything checked out. The contract was signed, and I now had a nice deposit in the bank. Best of all, the contents of an antebellum home waited to be scrutinized, categorized and stored. I would finally put that history degree to good use. No searching frantically for summer work. No more manning small-town Sno-Cone stands while wearing a goofy paper hat. Actually, that had been a fun job. Kids were my weakness and I had met plenty of them while I shoveled shaved ice and flavored syrups into cups.

With an even bigger smile, I remembered turning in my notice at the funeral home. Working in the records office wasn't creepy, but I'd felt continually surrounded by sadness. I dozed off in my quiet office during one boring, rainy afternoon and surprisingly had not dreamed a thing. *I guess the dead carry no memories. They leave them behind for people like me.*

My cell phone jangled on the seat next to me, and I tapped the ignore button. I was ultra-cautious when it came to driving, at least with the phone. Without looking, I knew it was William, mad and hurt that I had left him without a word. My frustration rose. He knew I was leaving, and I knew he didn't want me to go. What else was there to talk about?

I turned Natalie up louder and sang "Carnival" with all my heart.

Chapter 2

I had gotten on the road early, but there was no way I was driving eight hours straight. I couldn't sit still that long. I planned to stop in Green's Mill, Alabama, at a brand new bed and breakfast called the Delight of the South. The hotel's newness did not guarantee I would have a dream-free night, but I had a backup plan. I dug around blindly in my purse for the sleeping pills Dr. O'Neal had prescribed me. I was glad I'd remembered them, but I hated taking them. I always woke up feeling stupid, and the pills did not completely stop the dreams from coming. If the dream was there, I would still remember flashes of it the next day. But with sleeping pills, the dreams, unremembered and unappreciated faded quickly and settled back into the darkness.

I remembered the first time I took something to sleep. I would wake up screaming; masses of slithering snakes struggled to choke and strangle me in my dream, all because my mother, in a daze of medication or occasionally alcohol, had climbed in the bed with me to sleep. I could feel her loneliness, her confusion, her anger as she snored. At times I felt sorry for her, but then the snakes came while she slept. And in the daylight hours, the softness was gone.

I had plundered my mother's medicine cabinet and stolen one of her Valiums. "They always put her to sleep, so why not me?" my preteen self reasoned. I lingered on the memory, standing guiltily in front of that vanity mirror for a moment. I remembered thinking, "What would Jesus think about me stealing pills and doing drugs?" Hot tears had slid down my young face as I took the pill, choking it down without water.

Momma thought I was crazy, but the feeling was mutual. When I was about twelve, I'd tried to escape her cold indifference for a night by going to a neighbor's sleepover. I had felt safe and warm snuggled up with my sunny, red-haired friend Virginia. That night, Ginny had dreamed of her stepfather slipping into her room, sliding into her bed, lifting her pajamas and...

I was seized by Ginny's terror. I'd even felt her physical pain and woke up bathed in tears and blood. I had uncovered a tragic secret that would cost me a friendship. Even after Ginny's stepdad was arrested, I heard nothing from her. The unexpected twist was getting my first period, which had both confused and offended me. And I had made another discovery— screaming woke me from the nightmares that I witness occasionally.

I had not come home to find a sympathetic, benevolent mother. The short version of the story was Momma told her insipid religious friends that "Carrie Jo was psychic," and her prayer group tried to exorcise me. "Carrie Jo is full of the devil," Momma cried to anyone who would listen.

Momma never could keep a secret, not even her own. And she had plenty of them, I thought with a defiance and bitterness that almost smothered me.

Eventually, I wised up and kept my mouth shut about the dreams. If Momma and I had not moved around so much when I was growing up, I probably would have put those dream "demons" to sleep a bit easier. Instead, I slept in a constantly changing environment that included trailers, cheap motels and run-down homes most of my life until I left for college.

I shook my head to snap out of my reverie. I hated thinking about the past, but it chased me so much. I searched for a talk radio channel just to give myself something else to think about.

* * *

At lunch, I carried the binder of notes I had collected into a diner named Sal's and reread what I had been sent about my new project, Seven Sisters. I ordered a grilled cheese sandwich but sacrificially ignored the fries that came with it. I felt fat in my white shorts. They were a size ten, and I didn't want to move up to a twelve again. I had spent a lot of time walking the track near my home this past spring. I wasn't a big health nut, but I did like walking outdoors and exploring new scenery.

I smoothed my hand over the glossy picture of Seven Sisters, examining the columned facade of the main house. The antebellum home, the brief read, was built in 1823 by a family who went bankrupt shortly after the work was completed. By 1825, the wealthy Cottonwoods had purchased the mansion, renaming it Seven Sisters. Looking back at me from the collection of papers was a young woman with big, dark eyes, wearing a full-skirted gown with lace trim. She was riveting.

From what I had gathered from multiple video conferences and emails with the owner's attorney, the goal was to make Seven Sisters a sort of museum for visitors to Mobile, but the current owner had enough respect for the home's history to want a proper catalogue of its antiques first. That earned them points in my book. Too many people forget the past—I never could; it wouldn't allow me to.

I was the chief historian assigned to the project. I much preferred working alone, but that was impossible on a job this size. Luckily, my dearest friend and fellow historian, Mia, would be joining me soon. She had recommended me for the lead position, despite her own qualifications. She was one of the few people who knew about my "dream catching," as she called it. She never stayed in one spot too long—she had spent a few months in Egypt, then travelled to the UK for a tour of medieval castles, and then lived in Paris with a friend for six months over a bakery. I loved her confidence, her zest for life and her ability to travel like a local.

Mia knew more about antebellum artifacts than anyone I knew, which was hilarious considering Egyptology was her first love. I hadn't seen her since Christmas; I was excited to catch up on her latest adventures.

Right after college, I had worked on a few estate projects cataloging for an auction house. I was sad to see each antique sold off to the highest bidder. For a few months, I had possessed them, lovingly working to establish each item's value and historical importance. How I cried when the Trevi figurine, "Genteel Boy on Rocking Horse," sold at auction. The company had moved to Tennessee, and I had turned down an invitation to relocate with them. I'm not sure why.

I couldn't wait to see what Seven Sisters and Mobile had in store for me. Comparable to Charleston, Mobile had its charms; at least that's what the brochures told me. Coming so late in spring, I missed the city's big Mardi Gras party, but I wasn't much of a partier. I preferred studying the belongings of people who no longer walked the earth to drinking and dancing with its current residents.

I passed on a second glass of tea, as I didn't want to make another stop before calling it a day at the Delight of the South, but I gave the waitress a big smile all the same. I had a soft spot for hard-working women, having been one for so long.

I tucked a defiant curl behind my ear and flipped through the brief again. I would be working with Ashland Stuart, the current owner. His attorney had mailed me his picture and a brief summary of his credentials. He was incredibly handsome, in a masculine, southern kind of way. (*Too perfect. He must be short.*) He had short, blond hair with expressive blue eyes and a slightly pink, kissable mouth. I knew I had been staring too long at the photo because the waitress (Susan, according to her pink nametag) said, "Wow! He your boyfriend?"

"Nope, just a business partner." I smiled and flushed.

"Lucky girl." She tossed her head slightly in the direction of an open kitchen window at a heavyset man sweating over a grill. "He's my business partner." I laughed along with her but decided that was my cue to leave. I paid the bill, gathered the paperwork and left a nice tip for Susan. After she caught me leering at the picture of a complete stranger, it felt like passing off hush money.

Naturally, I thought of William, and I welcomed the guilt that seemed to surround everything in our relationship—or whatever it was. While the car's interior cooled off, I rang him back. His voicemail picked up, and I was so surprised that I stumbled over leaving a message.

"Hey, William, I'll be in Green's Mill soon. I'm doing fine, and the car is great. I wanted to say, I mean...I'll try to call again when I get to my room. Okay? Okay, talk to you later. Oh, this is Carrie Jo." Yep, that sounded dumb *and* guilty.

Chapter 3

My drive into Mobile was uneventful. Like most downtown areas, the streets were narrow and lumpy, and the roadways were shaded by the oak trees whose branches obscured the light with its boughs full of Spanish moss. I found my new garage apartment quite easily and spent a few minutes getting to know my temporary landlord, Bette. I knew right from that first meeting that I was going to like chatting with her. She was amiable and helpful, and she seemed to have a tremendous knowledge about the history of the area.

I spent some time getting my room in order. Time wasn't on my side; I had to get ready for an afternoon meeting with the attorney, the contractor and, of course, Ashland Stuart. The apartment was new, clean and completely comfortable. I adored it. Bette told me that she had considered writing a novel or two a few years ago, with the apartment as her studio, but life had not slowed enough so far to allow her the luxury. There was a full-size bed, complete with a comfortable mattress and clean cotton sheets. The desk was perched near the entrance window, which overlooked the street below and gave me a wonderful view of downtown. I was happy to see a mini-fridge and a kitchenette; Bette had really thought of all the basics. I decided to explore more later. Right now, I had a meeting to prepare for, and I was nervous already—I was the boss. I couldn't believe it! A few changes of clothes and about 45 minutes later, I was walking up to Seven Sisters.

I began to rethink my choice of shoes for the evening as I walked up the broken brick sidewalk that led to the house. Seven Sisters stood at the end of a private road that needed a bit of upkeep. As I walked, I breathed in the purple wisteria. Bees hung around it, even in the late afternoon, and the flowers drooped in the humidity. Tough brown vines grasped at any growing thing they could reach. Masses of pink azaleas that someone, years ago, thought would add color and charm to the sidewalk crowded the pathway.

Hollis Matthews, the attorney who had originally contacted me about the research project, had warned me about this slight inconvenience. But I had not realized I would be trekking through a subtropical jungle—not in these shoes, anyway. Silently, I rebuked myself. This was the opportunity of a lifetime! Was I going to let a little humidity and some abandoned gardens prevent me from exploring this prize?

As I moved along the path, I looked back at my blue car sitting behind a shiny black Lincoln with a few other vehicles—all the cars looked much nicer than mine. It suddenly occurred to me that I could afford to buy a new car now. My current employer was paying me well.

I smoothed my skirt, admiring the tiny red rose pattern, and tugged at my short-sleeved red blouse. The sweetheart neckline made me feel pretty and didn't reveal my cleavage at all. I touched my hair absently. It felt soft, but I knew the night air would make it curl even more. I had left my hair down for the evening, but I did manage to straighten it. Sort of. I at least made the effort to tame my normally wild locks.

I looked down at my worrisome shoes, red sandals with a pretty wedge heel, with my red painted toenails poking out happily. I decided I looked great, and I squared my shoulders to boost my confidence.

It was dusk, and the lights from the house shone through the thick hedges. The flowers' fragrance set an irresistible ambiance for a romantic southern evening. "How often does a girl get to visit an antebellum home that has been hidden away from the world for the past hundred years?" I asked myself. I felt very lucky indeed.

As the path turned, I stepped out of the maze of flowers, surprised at the sight of Seven Sisters, with her faded white columns rising up like an ancient Greek temple from the dark woods that surrounded her. I blinked, letting my eyes adjust to the fading light. The surrounding foliage and wild trees seemed to make it even darker. I stood gawking at my new office and felt no initial foreboding, no warning, just a warm feeling of delight and excitement. (I would reflect on this later. Shouldn't I have sensed something?) Oh yes, this would be my home—at least until next spring.

Through the old, warped windows, I could see lights and hear music playing softly inside. I hated being late and last. The scene seemed so strange, the present imposing on the past. Seven Sisters stood tall and silent, enduring the "party" that had gathered under her roof. The quiet dignity of the house juxtaposed against the tinkling of laughter and the sounds of jazz music made the gathering seem like a group of naughty teenagers assembled to dance on a grave, disregarding all the lost life beneath their feet.

The warm feeling from just a moment ago disappeared as the fine hairs on my neck pricked up. Suddenly, I felt the air move slightly. I scanned the area around me but detected only an abandoned garden statue a few yards away. It was an odd—and disturbing—sight. The statue was a satyr pouring water over a nude girl. His tongue poked out at me, the one who dared invade his garden. His grotesque face, as well as the rest of him, was weathered green, evidence of his lengthy stay on the property. I laughed nervously, pulling my attention away from the leering creature. I paused on the sparse grass below the steps leading to the great house. A curious aroma of damp, old wood and leaves filled the air, and I could see that the promised repairs had begun with the wooden porch. Out of the corner of my eye, I detected movement. I turned quickly, my skirt swirling around my tanned legs.

A broad white smile and the handsome face of Ashland Stuart greeted me. He wasn't short—at all.

"Hey! I hope I didn't startle you." Ashland smiled even bigger, if that were possible. For some reason, I was not sure he was honest in his apology. He looked like someone who liked having the upper hand.

"Well, maybe a little. I didn't hear you pull up." I smiled back nervously and purposefully turned my attention back to the house, away from the man who had managed to sneak up on me. I needed a moment to compose myself.

"I'm Ashland Stuart, but I'm sure you know that—my attorney believes in bios with pictures. I recognize you from yours, Carrie Jo Jardine." I didn't know what to say; he seemed to know everything. So I gave him a slight nod. He stood close to me and turned his attention to the house. "First time here at Seven Sisters?"

"Yes. I regret that my maiden voyage had to be in the dark. Still, I'm glad to be here. Can I ask you a question?"

His white teeth gleamed at me; they shone in the fading light, making him look like something fierce. He had a wide, masculine smile, which I suspected he enjoyed flashing at all the women he encountered. "Any question at all."

I ignored his flirtatious invitation. "Seven Sisters—how did it get its name? It's easy to romanticize a name like that, so I figured I'd ask someone who probably knows rather than assume it was named after seven actual sisters or a family of tragic Greek goddesses. There were no real facts on that in the profile I received."

He laughed at that, and then it was my turn to smile at him. "Not a romantic, then? Actually, we're not sure and had hoped that our new historian would be able to answer that question for us in the fullness of time." He shot me another smile. "Family gossip suggests that the Seven Sisters are actually the seven columns that surround the house. But there are those who think it may be a clue to a lost family treasure."

"How interesting," I said sincerely, captivated by the notion of uncovering a family secret.

"One other older bit of gossip is that Seven Sisters is not this house at all but the name of the family house in France. That was the talk in the 1820s, anyway. Who knows? Perhaps you'll be able to settle it once and for all." I didn't know what to say, but I was intrigued.

He broke the silence. "It looks like we're both late. I've kept you to myself for too long." He stood so close I could smell his expensive cologne. It was worth the money. I had an urge to touch his creased cotton shirt. I snuck a peek up at him as he stood silently gazing at Seven Sisters.

I wondered what he dreamt about when he closed his light blue eyes at night. Would he see memories of a happy childhood, inspiring dreams tinged in a warm, honey hue, or would his dreams unroll endlessly like dark shadows leaking from a deadly, hidden personality? There was only one way to truly know, and I shuddered slightly at the thought of waking up next to this golden man.

He must have felt my movement as I sensed my own terrible vulnerability, standing in the woods, in the dark, with a man I did not know. He looked at me serenely, like another statue in the garden. Only he was much nicer to look at than the satyr. I felt like he belonged here.

"Shall we make a grand entrance?" He offered me his arm, as I suspected he had done with countless women before me. Feeling disarmed, as much by my own thoughts as by his practiced charm, I nodded courteously and looped my arm through his, trying to ignore his muscles. I shoved back conjured images of southern belles entertaining well-dressed suitors as they glided up these same steps together before walking through the massive doors of the house. (I wasn't a romantic, right?) My skin flushed slightly, and I didn't know if it was due to my nerves or the nearness of Ashland Stuart.

He rang the bell, and the door swung open. We were greeted by a tall, distinguished-looking man who I knew immediately was Hollis Matthews, Ashland's attorney. Before I could speak, Ashland said, "Look who I found wandering around the property." He gave me a playful grin as he strode down the hall, and I took a moment to admire his big shoulders. Matthews was a perfectly dressed gentleman, down to his blue suit with a subtle pinstripe, white pocket handkerchief and neat manicure.

"Not wandering, just walking up the driveway," I called after Ashland. I fought my natural tendency to get defensive when embarrassed. "You must be Mr. Matthews." I leaned forward to shake the attorney's hand, remembering to act like a professional. His skin felt cool and moist, and I wanted to snatch my hand away and wipe it on my skirt. With a tiny nod, he welcomed me inside the foyer of Seven Sisters.

I couldn't resist a good stare at my surroundings. I was delighted to see that repairs had begun in earnest, but there was much more to do. It was much as I expected: wooden wall panels hidden under peeling paint and misapplied wallpaper, and bare wooden floors that looked spongy in a few places. A sprawling staircase filled the center of the room, and off to either side, I could see many rooms with darkened doorways. A collection of boxes and crates lined the foyer, and I felt a flurry of nerves and excitement. I could hardly believe I was the boss. Well, the boss of the museum project, anyway. Something told me that the sleek Mr. Matthews may have been the true man in charge here.

"Miss Jardine, it's such a pleasure to meet you. I hope that driveway didn't give you too much trouble. We'll make it proper soon. Kindly step this way; I've got a few things for you to sign. I hope you like the arrangements we made for you. Our contractor has been working around the clock to get your rooms ready."

"I think there's been some kind of mistake. I did not plan on staying on-site. I've already rented a small apartment just a half mile away. I just have…I have certain…"

"Didn't you?" He slid his silver glasses down his thin nose and walked toward a small table and overstuffed chairs near a dusty fireplace. I followed him to continue my protest and immediately began a mental appraisal of the items in the room while he shuffled through a stack of papers.

"It's Carrie Jo, please." I took a step toward the cabinet, unable to resist a peek. "When will I be able to start?"

"Soon. First, I need you to sign this confidentiality agreement, the one we discussed on the phone. It's fairly standard, but please let me know if you have any questions. You can start as soon as you like. As soon as tomorrow, of course. With such eagerness to explore this mansion-sized time capsule, I'm surprised you wouldn't like to stay. Aren't historians slaves to history?" Without waiting for a reply, he continued, "We've arranged for you to have a room here, along with your team." Matthews slid the papers and a pen across the table and appraised me. He had slate gray eyes, almost as shiny as his glasses.

"I sure hate to inconvenience you, but I won't be staying on-site." I felt my backbone stiffen slightly as I sat opposite him, faking confidence. "I hope that's not a problem for you or Mr. Stuart."

"It's not a condition, of course, and we do realize you can't devote yourself to this project around the clock. The offer was meant to help you offset some costs and make things more convenient, but it's whatever you desire." He accepted my signed papers and passed me an envelope with a check inside. I slid the check into my red clutch without even looking at the numbers. Such a fastidious man. He would never miss a small thing like a zero.

He smiled and rose from his chair. "Well, Miss Jardine. That is, Carrie Jo. Let's take that tour. I'm sure you are eager to meet the contractor." He pointed me back toward the door.

I listened to him talk about the upcoming maintenance schedule as we walked down the hall to the back of the house. I wanted to yell "Stop!" at every door we passed, but I figured I could control my curiosity just this once.

"Mind your step on the..."

I felt a sharp, stabbing pain at the back of my head. Everything went black, then fuzzy, and then slowly the lights came on. It was as if someone had hit a dimmer switch. What had been there before, a dark, empty hallway with peeling paint and an inch of dust on the chair arms, had transformed. The paint looked fresh, a pale blue, and the wooden baseboards shone with wax. Fine wooden floors lined with blue floral-patterned runners looked vibrant and soft. A long table against the wall held trays of fresh fruit and hot foods. Lined up against the wall were three young black men holding trays and pitchers, wearing white collared shirts and black cotton pants. I drew my breath sharply, surprised by their frozen presence and glad they didn't seem to see me sprawled on the floor even though I was practically under their feet.

I realized that somehow, I was having a genuine Carrie Jo dream.

Chapter 4

The heat from Muncie's starched white collar comforted him on this unusually cool October evening. Seven Sisters was full of candles and laughter, and it smelled like a banquet, just like one he had heard about in a fairy story. In the distance, the boy heard the deep, booming voice of Stokes, the house man, announcing supper to the guests. Muncie held the silver tray tightly—a neat trick while wearing thick, white cotton gloves. All serving slaves wore white gloves. Mr. Cottonwood would be mightily embarrassed to serve his guests food that slaves had been dipping their hands in. Best to keep the gloves on to show you had clean hands.

It took skill to keep those gloves clean and white during service, to walk in the stiff shoes, to tote a tray without clattering a spoon. Muncie had kept Early and the other boys up half the night walking the space of their small room until Stokes poked his head in and told him to go to bed. He wanted to practice; he didn't dare trip and fall on his face.

Muncie's heart pounded in his chest, and his dark skin flushed with excitement. Stokes strode to the servants' hall, inspecting each of the gathered slaves. Muncie kept his eyes down respectfully, staring at his own reflection in the shiny tray. He bit the inside of his lip to stop himself from smiling. He hardly ever saw himself, except when he could slip off to the river. There were plenty of mirrors in Seven Sisters, but he could get smacked for looking too long in any of them. It was too late in the year to swim now.

His first night of dinner service seemed like a dream. Really, he was too young to serve, but he was tall. And Hooney, the missus' housemaid, said he was pleasing to the eye even though he was very dark.

Early hadn't lasted in service. Muncie didn't know if Early had clattered spoons or gawked too much at the guests or spoken out of turn. Besides the beating he took, the older boy seemed relieved to leave the dining hall. He had no stomach for killing chickens and wearing shoes. He preferred spending his time fishing with Mr. Cottonwood or traveling with him into Mobile. Early didn't care; he was happy. That made Muncie feel a bit better about taking his spot.

Tonight was a special night. A bunch of people he didn't know were coming to dine with the Cottonwoods. In this little corner of what Muncie knew was a big world, the Cottonwoods meant everything to the plantation families of Old Mobile. Mrs. Cottonwood lay upstairs in her birthing bed, where she would stay until the baby arrived. She had a kind face and soft hands and had soothed his head once when he was full of the fever. Even though that was many years ago, Muncie remembered her cool touch and kind care. Now his friend Calpurnia was mistress of Seven Sisters, at least until Mrs. Cottonwood had the baby, since Mr. Cottonwood was often away. Calpurnia meant the world to Muncie, but she was also old enough to get married. Some gentlemen, both young gentlemen and some older men, were coming now from miles around to take a peek at Calpurnia. He didn't know how he felt about that, but mostly, he didn't think about it. There was always something to do nowadays.

Tonight, Calpurnia's cousin Isla, her uncle Louis and a group of neighbors filled Seven Sisters to capacity. Calpurnia had told him that she didn't really want to have this party and that she'd rather stay with her mother. She was nervous about the whole thing, and he wanted to make her proud. He loved Calpurnia, not like Tristan loved Isolde but like she was his own blood, like she was his kin. The very thought made Muncie blush again.

Besides the chatting of the people he served, the house seemed quiet after the business of the day. A stream of slaves had flowed from the main house to the cook house like a line of busy ants. Some toted water for baths; others carried trays of fruit and bottles of wine. When the hot food came to the house, two small boys ran out in front, tossing balls of hot cornbread at the hounds, shouting, "Hush puppy! Hush puppy!" Those pups couldn't resist those treats. Once they gobbled them up, they were easily wrangled and taken away from the house before the dinner guests sat down. Nobody wanted to hear a pack of yapping dogs while they ate their dinner. That's what Stokes said, although Muncie knew for a fact he was fond of those animals.

Suddenly, the guests came flooding into the room like magical creatures on mists of perfume. The ladies, most of whom Muncie didn't recognize, wore dresses so big that the skirts swirled about them like colorful clouds. Some were made of colors he had never seen. He resisted the urge to touch the airy fabrics.

All of the gentlemen looked stiff and straight with high white collars and tapered cloaks, like the toy soldiers Muncie found stuffed in a box in the upstairs nursery a long time ago. Even Mr. Cottonwood looked clean and nice, like he'd been dipped in the Mobile River six or seven times. Tall Uncle Louis had white teeth that shone all the time, maybe because he smiled all the time. Muncie searched the crowd but did not see Calpurnia. He heard a nearby sniff and realized he was gawking. He didn't dare to look at Stokes, instead shifting his eyes downward to his tray.

Stokes strode past him and the other slaves and walked to the wooden double doors of the dining hall. Standing tall and straight, he announced in his deepest voice, "Ladies and gentlemen, I present to you Miss Calpurnia Cottonwood of Mobile and Miss Isla Torrence of Savannah."

Feeling safe with Stokes at such a distance, Muncie peeked at the door. The two girls strode into the room together, arm in arm like two roses of different colors. Isla turned her head to cast her broad smile around the room—a move that seemed bold, beyond her fifteen years. Her blond curls bounced like they were happy too. Perky dimples showed brightly in her soft pink cheeks. Muncie could see, even in the failing light, that her eyes glistened with pleasure at all the attention.

Muncie's heart sank when he saw his friend. Although she wore a small smile and tipped her head slightly at a few of the guests, her unhappiness was obvious to anyone with eyes. Taller than her cousin and thinner by far, Calpurnia looked like a queen, like Guinevere, without even trying. Her soft brown hair was piled high on her head with pretty combs tucked in the silky tresses. Coral earrings dangled from her ears; Muncie recognized them as Mrs. Cottonwood's.

The gathered guests clapped appreciatively, and the ladies took a turn around the room and were seated on either side of Mr. Cottonwood at the head of the table. When Calpurnia sat down, Muncie could see her cheeks flush under all the attention. He knew she would rather be in the library or tugging at flowers and weeds or at her mother's bedside—anywhere but there.

For the next hour, Muncie was too fearful to think of Miss Calpurnia, even though she was very close. He catered to Stokes' every need and snapped to attention when summoned. It took all the discipline he had not to look interested in the conversations that teemed around the table, although he and the other slaves were very busy. Occasionally, he tossed a suspicious, disapproving look at one tall, dark-haired gentleman sitting a little too close to Calpurnia. Captain Garrett was his name. He had been here before and had taken Calpurnia on an unchaperoned stroll around the side garden. He insisted on pouring her drink and asked her questions that didn't seem to be any of his business.

Muncie was relieved, for more than one reason, when the dinner service came to an end.

After dinner, the gentlemen would find a fine Kentucky whiskey waiting for them in the front parlor while the ladies would take lemonade, with gin if they chose, on the side porch. Musicians played softly in the background, and heaps of flowers on the mantelpieces and tables filled the dining hall with a heavy fragrance of magnolias, honeysuckle and beeswax.

Muncie wished he could pat Calpurnia's hand and assure her that she was lovely and perfect. She would agonize later over every detail. Trying to get to Calpurnia nowadays to speak with her or just be with her had proven difficult. Every time he tried to walk with her in the grove or meet her near the gardens, he had met Isla instead. She seemed to know his every move, and even now as she left the dining hall, he felt her eyes on him. He blushed against his collar, now wet with sweat.

Isla had been at Seven Sisters only two weeks, but she acted as if she were the lady of the house. According to Hooney, the girl was putting on airs because everyone, even the house slaves, knew "that she was just a poor relation of no true standing."

The day before the party, she had taken a fall near the fountains. At first, Muncie had felt alarmed when he saw her lying on the ground. She'd cried and cried, and he was worried that she had been hurt. But once he got there, he suspected she just wanted him to hold her. "Hold me, Muncie! No, don't leave me here," she had murmured like she was beginning to faint.

Normally, he wouldn't touch her, but he didn't dare leave her stranded in the yard either. As he had lifted her in his arms, she'd smelled like honeysuckle and stolen sweets. Feeling her soft little arms around his neck made him feel strong, like a man. But a greater, deeper fear gripped him inside. Instead of loving Isla, loving holding the frail little creature that clung to him too tightly, he couldn't wait to deliver his misbegotten goods to someone else. He had called out to the house as he approached, "Mister Stokes, Mister Stokes, sir!"

Isla had protested angrily, saying he was walking too fast, but he'd ignored the feeling of her frilly clothes crushed under his hands and her girlish voice. He'd held her like she was a snake, a dangerous snake—like one of those black snakes that chased you with all their might until you began chasing them back. In this case, that didn't seem like a good idea. He had done right in calling out, Stokes had said, but he must never again touch any of the women in the house. Not even if she fell down a well. Stokes had called him stupid, but Hooney had understood. Muncie hadn't told anyone else, not even Calpurnia.

Muncie relinquished his silver tray at the waiting station and dabbed his forehead and neck with a towel. His breakfast was long gone, and he heard his stomach rumbling. But he shuffled after Stokes in his clunky shoes, ready to serve the men in the study. Mostly, he was supposed to watch and learn, but he had to be ready to help out if called on. So far, nothing exciting had happened. Mr. Cottonwood and Captain Garrett talked loudly about traffic along the Mobile River while the Cottonwoods' neighbors, Mr. Semmes and Mr. Beauchamp, exchanged jokes that Muncie didn't understand and then slapped one another on the back. Captain Garrett laughed too loudly, and it seemed he liked pouring Mr. Cottonwood his whiskey.

A light tap on the door surprised Muncie, and he hustled through the opening to see who was beckoning to him. Moving as fast as lightning and waving to him was Isla. "Muncie!"

A jolt of worry hit his stomach, and this time he knew it wasn't a rumble of hunger. His brain yelled "Danger!"

but he worried that something was wrong with Calpurnia. Against his better judgment, he slipped into the Blue Room, next to the men's parlor, behind her. It was dark except for a single candelabrum that shone like a faraway beacon near the window.

Before he knew what was happening, Isla melted her body against his and planted her lips on his dry mouth.

Her kiss was delicious and tasted like lemonade. She made a little groan against him, shaking him back to reality, and he pushed her, holding her at arm's length away from him. He didn't know what to say except, "Please…" In a second, her inviting lips curled tightly in a rueful scowl, and her body stiffened. She suddenly seemed tall and imposing, not soft and pliable as she had been seconds before.

With savage ferocity, she slapped him across the face, stinging his cheek and his still-warm lips. "I know the truth about you, Muncie! You don't think I see how you moon after Calpurnia like a whipped dog?" Her voice was a seething whisper. She stepped even farther away from him, peering at him. "She's no better than me, even though she has a rich daddy and an old name. You'll see, Muncie. You'll see who the real woman is." With that, she swished out of the Blue Room with a click of her heels. Muncie touched his hand to his cheek, still hot from Isla's vicious slap….

Chapter 5

"Carrie Jo! Can you hear me?"

"Miss Jardine, we've called an ambulance. They'll be here momentarily." Matthews spoke very close to my ear; his stale breath brushed my skin—too intimately for my taste.

I shook my head. "No, just give me a minute." My weak protest started a hushed conversation, but I was simply too tired to eavesdrop. Snippets of my dream— the crushed white magnolias on the mantelpiece, the coral earrings that hung from Calpurnia's slender ears— crowded into my mind. The scent of hot cornbread, the taste of lemonade on my lips and the warm aroma of clean beeswax lingered on and around me like an invisible cloud. As always, I was surprised no one else could taste and see these things. Unwanted tears slid down my cheeks. Muncie's hopeful face hovered before me. He was dead, long dead. He would never know that I had been there, witnessing a day in his private life.

"Here, put your arms around my neck. You can do that, right? You can't just lie here on the floor."

I slid my arms around Ashland's neck and laid my throbbing head on his shoulder. "But I barely even know you," I whispered.

He laughed softly and said, "You're going to be fine," as if his words would fix everything. He carefully positioned me on an antique settee near the window in the front room, where I had met Matthews earlier. "I'll be right back. Don't go anywhere," Ashland said with a smile.

I had to chuckle. *Here I am, lying helpless on a fainting couch.*

Matthews looked down at me with his piercing, gray eyes. "I've called the family's physician, Dr. Patterson. He'll be here in just a minute. No arguments on this. You'll understand that I can't have you knocking yourself out without some follow-up medical care."

I nodded and wiped away the unexpected damp streaks on my face. "Of course."

Ashland reappeared with some bandages. With a quick, "This might hurt," he pressed them to the screaming spot on my head. I focused on the darkness outside the window, dutifully accepting his attempts at healing. The doorbell rang, and the sleek attorney disappeared down the hallway.

"Looks like it stopped bleeding," Ashland said. "That's always a good sign." He pulled my hand up to hold the bandages in place while he cleaned up the paper wrappings.

"Good evening, Ashland. Miss Jardine, is it? Now let's take a look." Matthews was thin, but Dr. Patterson made him look muscular in comparison. The doctor probed my scalp with a bony finger, examining the wound without a lot of fuss. I bit my lip to stop from shouting during his inspection. He sat next to me, flashed a light in my eyes and checked my pulse. "So tell me about this fall. Was it from a great height?" Before I could answer, Matthews spoke. "Actually, she tripped over a bit of old carpet. No great height at all."

"Can you follow my finger, please?" Obediently, I followed the doctor's bony finger as he moved it back and forth in front of my face. "Well, Matthews, I think she'll be just fine. It wouldn't hurt to get a stitch or two, but you will certainly live." He stared up at Matthews, who said nothing. He peered at me over the top of his glasses. "Do you feel nauseous? Can you stand, Miss Jardine?"

I was determined to get on my feet. This couldn't be happening. "I feel fine, truly. Embarrassed, mostly. I'm sure I can stand up."

"Hold on. Take your time, darling. You don't want to get ahead of yourself. If you do feel sick or off-balance at all, go to the hospital. It's possible that a whack like that could cause a concussion, but I expect you're fine. Ashland, help her up, please." The friendly doctor watched me amble about for a moment before declaring me healed.

"Do you have a friend who can drive you home? I'd feel better knowing you were tucked in safely for the night. Is there some family close by?" The doctor removed his glasses, polishing them with a shirt sleeve before replacing them, without much improvement. He looked at me inquisitively.

"Uh, no, I've no family here. But my place is just a few minutes away. I'm really very embarrassed to have made such a scene."

"Well, accidents happen, and it's not surprising in a place as old as this. I'm sure there are all kinds of hazards around here." He looked at Ashland with a grin and said, "It's good that someone is going to restore her. Seven Sisters, I mean. She must have been a beauty in her day." Bag in hand, the doctor glanced around the room for a moment, then handed me his card. "Now you call me if you have any problems at all tonight. If I'm not in, my wife will take a message. If you folks don't need anything else from me, I'll be off. I do expect you to call tomorrow, perhaps when you finish here, okay?"

"Thank you, Dr. Patterson. I'll walk you to the door." Matthews led the doctor from the room, and I was left with my boss watching over me as I sat on the dusty couch.

Once Ashland and I were alone, my face flushed. I felt like an incompetent ninny falling down in front of the great football hero. What must he think of me? Why did I care? I felt raw emotions building just below the surface and knew I would need some privacy to recall what I had seen and experienced without the added embarrassment of an audience. Like a cornered rabbit, I was ready to run. It was always that way after a dream. It was almost like I had too many feelings; they piled up on one another in a big old heap.

"I think I'll go back to my apartment now. I've had enough fun for one night. I'm sorry I messed up the meeting."

"Don't worry about that. You heard the doctor, though. You shouldn't drive, Carrie Jo. I'll take you home. You say it's not far?"

"No, it's not far, over near Catherine Street, but I don't want to leave my car here. And I don't want to be any more trouble." I tried to think of a good reason to refuse but couldn't really find one beyond leaving my car behind.

"It's the least I can do. You did trip on my property. I'll take you home, and then either Matthews or I can bring your car to you later. Let's find your things. And I'll need those keys."

He sounded so assured and logical that I didn't put up a fight. I forced Muncie out of my mind and set about looking for my purse and keys. I found them on the desk in the front room with the check I had so happily received earlier.

The ride home was quiet and short, only three turns. On a sunny day, I could make the walk from Seven Sisters to the garage apartment in about ten minutes, I figured. I looked forward to that. The roads were uneven and dark, despite the many streetlights. Most of the downtown streets I had seen were shrouded in live oaks, giving the whole area a sort of otherworldly feel. *No wonder I'm dreaming of the old days*, I thought wryly. *I'm surrounded by history.*

I was thankful Ashland hadn't encroached on my silence. It took a lot of effort to not rewind the dream in his presence, slowly, carefully, reliving each detail. I wanted to remember everything, blurt it all out, but the wisest choice was to capture it all in my digital journal. I shuddered to think of how Ashland would look at me if he knew about my "dream catching." I didn't want to find out with this throbbing head. It would be a long night.

We pulled into the gravel driveway, and I fumbled for the apartment key. Without asking, he stepped out of the car, opening the car door without a word. I was relieved to find that climbing the stairs to the apartment went easily. No repeat performances; no falls.

"Thank you for bringing me home."

"No trouble at all. We'll bring your car back in a few minutes. I'll put your keys in the planter here." He looked at me steadily. "I'm sure you want to clean up a bit. Call Dr. Patterson if you have any problems at all. He's on call 24/7. Is there anything else you need? Are you sure you're okay? Do you want me to bring you some supper?"

"Thanks, but I'm not really hungry. I think I have something to snack on in the fridge. I appreciate you bringing me home. Thank you again."

Flashing his easy smile, he left me on the porch. I slid the key into the lock, and then I was finally inside, alone, leaning against the door. No brave face needed. Nothing to prove—and after all that, no flow of tears.

I pulled off the offending shoes and decided against tossing them into the trash can near my desk. They weren't to blame, although I doubted I would have the confidence to wear them again anytime soon. Locking the door and checking the shades, I tossed a scoop of bath salts into warm running water and soaked in the tub for the next twenty minutes. I carefully avoided putting pressure on my head; I leaned back into the water, feeling it soothe away the tension. After a few minutes, the details of the dream came back, slowly at first and then like a flood. From the yapping hounds to the feel of stiff cotton on my neck, I recalled the details with surreal clarity. Unwilling to lose even a snippet, I climbed out of the tub and wrapped myself in a cotton robe, half drying my tired body. I didn't want to peek at my head. I hated the sight of blood.

I took a bottle of water from the mini-fridge and went over to the laptop on the desk, flipping it on. My fingers flew over the keyboard as I wrote down my dream, scene by scene. Like a supernatural scribe, I obediently recorded all I had witnessed. It was a habit I had developed over the years, first in book journals and then on my computers. It was a weird sort of record, a kind of written proof that I wasn't crazy. It felt like I was collecting evidence for a case that I hoped one day to present to someone who might actually understand. As usual, I finished with a brief commentary of what I felt during the dream and after.

Hours later, I cried. Too tired to write anymore, I shuffled to the full-size bed. It took up half of the apartment, but I was grateful for the comfort. I slid out of the robe, tossed on a giant sleep shirt and peeled back the sheets. I reached my hand under the cheap bamboo paper lampshade and clicked the light off. Drained and tired, and finally empty of borrowed memories, I slept like the dead.

Chapter 6

I awoke later than I had planned, but I felt excited about the day ahead of me. My new landlord, Bette, had politely tapped on my door to invite me to breakfast, an unexpected perk that I sincerely appreciated. I stepped into the bright kitchen of Bette's home to eat a bowl of decadent cheesy grits and bacon. The smell set my stomach to growling. The kitchen had an old-fashioned but tidy floor and a vintage, chrome-edged table. A bowl of polished wax fruit decorated the tabletop, along with a pair of whimsical Campbell's Soup salt and pepper shakers. *This is what a home must feel like,* I thought happily.

"Ready to work on that big old house today?" Bette slid a small glass of juice and a cup of coffee toward me, and I gratefully accepted them.

"Yes, I think I am! It's going to be a lot of work, but chances like this don't come but once in a lifetime, really. Thanks again for allowing me to stay in the apartment."

"Oh, it's my treat. I like having people nearby, and frankly, I'm happy that Mr. Stuart has hired you. They needed to do something about that place. The Seven Sisters mansion is too beautiful to just rot into the landscape; we Mobilians need to have a bit more pride in our history here. We've got some real stories to tell. Did you know that the French settlers used to send little orphan girls over here to marry these backwoods French-Canadians? Poor little things. They called them the Pelican Girls because they landed on Dauphin Island in Pelican Bay. No, wait, maybe the ship was called The Pelican. Oh, I can't remember, but there are plenty of sad stories to tell. Not the least of which are the ones from Seven Sisters, but I guess you know all about those." Bette's short white curls framed her round face perfectly and shook with her expressiveness.

"I don't know a thing, really—only the facts from the brochures. I am intrigued, though." Then I thought for a moment and asked, "Are the Stuarts an old family here in Mobile?"

Bette smiled, then launched into her story. "Well, Mrs. Stuart was actually a Hunter. They were the ones who purchased Seven Sisters sometime in the 1960s. According to my friend, Cynthia Dowd—she's on the board of the Historical Society, and she has such lovely white hair—the families here were very excited when the Hunters purchased the property. There was a lot of work going on at Oakleigh, the antebellum over off Government Boulevard. People had hoped that the Hunters would do the same thing with Seven Sisters, but nothing happened. Emily Stuart died sometime around 1985, I think. After that, things just quieted down. That was such a sad affair. That little boy, Ashland, was so brave. He didn't have a soul to depend on. Not counting all the family that came out of the woodwork. Imagine, so young and so much money, of course. Still he's got a good head on his shoulders. Cynthia has bent over backwards to introduce him to her daughter—poor cross-eyed girl. He's come to a few of our luncheons and talked about the old house. What a stir he caused. I can't understand why he's not married yet." Bette sipped her coffee from the chipped china cup and stood to look out the window.

Before I could ask anything else, the cuckoo clock on the wall signaled the half hour, kicking me into business mode. "I have to run. I can't be late, not good for the first day on a new job. Is there anything I can do to help clean up?" I rose from the vinyl-padded chair and carried my dishes to the sink. I wasn't used to anyone cooking for me, much less washing my dishes.

"Oh, no. I've got this little meal under control. I'll make biscuits tomorrow. Maybe you'll tell me what you find. I wish I could explore that old home. Such sadness, I bet."

I waved goodbye and stepped outside into the sunshine. I had dressed in comfortable, light clothing, just blue jeans, a new T-shirt and sneakers. That was a good thing. It was warm already, and I imagined it would get even warmer in the house. I managed to pull my hair back in a ponytail, partly because I wanted to hide last night's wound and partly because I knew I'd sweat.

Last night's accidental dream already seemed like a distant memory, but I didn't doubt that Muncie had lived, served and maybe died right where I would be working. Finding out more about him was added incentive to dig deep into the history of the old home. It felt good to have a purpose beyond cataloging antiques and paintings.

My phone jangled in my purse. I pulled it out and sighed. William. I couldn't keep putting off talking to him; it just never seemed like a good time. That described our relationship perfectly—off-balance and never right. I couldn't blame him entirely. He tried to make me happy, but I had to be honest. I didn't love him. With a sigh, I hit the ignore button. I found my car keys in the planter where Ashland had promised to leave them. I knew that he had driven my car home. When I opened the door, I caught a whiff of his cologne. Absently, I wondered if I would see him today as I eased out of the driveway.

When I arrived, I was on time but nearly last to the party. The small road that led to the house was lined with work trucks, everything from landscapers to a local computer setup team. It was weird knowing that many of these contractors waited on directions from me. I grabbed my laptop bag, along with my notes, and headed up the path. It was nice to make the trek in the daylight. (I intended on sticking my tongue out at the ugly satyr.)

Walking through the azalea-lined pathway seemed much less menacing with a blue sky trying to peep through. A squirrel squeaked and skittered in the underbrush, probably complaining at the cacophony of humans who disturbed his normally peaceful environment. "Sorry, little guy," I said with a shrug.

At the end of the path I once again faced Seven Sisters, my new second home, and the sheer size of the building set me back on my heels. The house sat slightly to the right of the path. I could plainly see the work that time had so mercilessly made of the house, the missing and hanging plantation shutters, the moss covering everything that dared reach up for the sun. Fruit and pecan trees that had begun as hopeful saplings now smothered the landscape, closing in perilously on the house. Off to the right of the path stood several statues, including the revolting satyr who had mocked me the night before. I spied a brick walkway under a collection of leaves. I was happy to see the landscaping company taking the initiative, cleaning up the limbs and leaves scattered on the ground. I gave a wave in their direction, mentally pledging to talk with them later.

I didn't stop at the steps this time but walked right in like I owned the place. I found Matthews, sleeves rolled up and sweat on his brow, helping a young man open boxes in the front room. "Good morning!" I said cheerily, my ponytail swinging as I jumped in to help. After a brief discussion, I persuaded Matthews to allow me to relocate the computers for the inventory system to the back of the house. I reasoned that it would be cooler and, since I would later be working on the back of the property, in various sheds and buildings, more convenient for my team and me. Less walking and hauling around expensive equipment, I said. Truthfully, I think I just wanted to be in the Blue Room. Close to Muncie.

I met the general contractor, Terrence Dale, who insisted I call him TD. He was handsome in an earthy sort of way. He had lively brown eyes and a natural enthusiasm about life that was infectious. He seemed as excited as I was about restoring the home. Both of us were young and ready to earn our place in our respective arenas. According to him, he had fought long and hard to win the contract. With the recommendation of the Historical Society, he ultimately dominated the competition. He was only a little older than me, probably not thirty yet, but he had already worked on several local projects. I liked TD immediately and was glad to work with someone so knowledgeable and amiable. My part of the remodel would be only as a historical consultant, which left me with plenty of time to stay focused on my task. I couldn't wait to get my hands dirty.

After hours of setting up passwords and permissions on the computer network, checking delivery dates and sending introductory emails, I begged off lunch and slipped away to take my own private tour of Seven Sisters, before the full team arrived and the hard work began. I wanted to feel the place, to reconnect with the past. Don't get me wrong—I'm not a psychic, but I don't claim to understand how my dream life really works. My goal wasn't just to give my client a catalog of inventory. I wanted to quietly honor and pay homage to the people who had once loved all these things. I'd already walked through much of the ground floor during the course of the day, including the Blue Room, the banquet hall, the massive ballroom and the two front parlors, but now I could take my time, free from questions and Hollis Matthews' invading stare.

Chapter 7

I had spent considerable time in the ladies' parlor the evening before. Like the rest of the house, it had high, smooth ceilings with intricate wood trim. A massive sliding wooden door, with a convenient keyhole peephole, separated it from the men's parlor. The peephole opened only from the men's side.

The men's parlor had a small fireplace and a wall lined with built-in bookshelves. If I closed my eyes, I could smell the faint aroma of pipe tobacco that had once, many years ago, filled this dark paneled room in celebration of Miss Calpurnia Cottonwood. I hoped that somewhere in the house, those books had been found. Both parlors had doors that opened to a wide porch. The sliding door that connected to the Blue Room was less impressive. The Blue Room was slightly larger than the other two parlors. During Muncie's time, the windows were hung with heavy blue curtains embellished with gold threads. Now they stood bare, naked. Despite the warm afternoon, I shivered. Walking to the alcove where I had witnessed the unwanted kiss, I amateurishly attempted to open myself emotionally to feel a remnant of life, to experience the boy's turmoil again. But I felt nothing, only sadness at seeing a veil of dirt on the wall and grooves in the wooden floor made by dragging heavy furniture.

According to TD, Seven Sisters was at first built in a T-shaped, Greek Revival style, perfect for keeping the home cool even during Mobile's hottest subtropical summers. Over time, rooms had been added, expanding the size of the home for entertaining. I longed to open the doors and windows and allow fresh air to flow through the home. I promised myself I would do that someday. I strolled down the hall to the room where I had witnessed the house slaves lining up for inspection. It was smaller than the rest of the rooms, and it also had a sliding door that connected it to the music room. Just beyond that, at the front of the house, was the banquet hall. None of the original furniture remained on-site, but I had some leads on the table.

My stomach rumbled, and I glanced at my watch. It was past one; Chip, the IT guy, the maintenance team and Hollis Matthews would undoubtedly be returning from lunch at Mama's, a nearby eatery on Dauphin Street. I secretly hoped that they had ignored my earlier protest and had taken the initiative to bring me back a snack, but I didn't count on it.

I felt in my pocket for my tiny but powerful LED flashlight and climbed up the wooden staircase. The contractor had assured me that the staircase was in good condition and could be safely used. The occasional twinge on my scalp hoped he knew what he was talking about.

I stepped lightly on the bare wooden floors, ignoring the squeaks and complaints of the old staircase. My sweaty ponytail hung limp in the stifling heat of the upper floor. TD promised that cool air would be flowing up here by tomorrow, and I hoped he was right. I couldn't ask my team to work in this oppressive heat. I quickly climbed to the top of the stairs and walked to the two large windowed doors that overlooked the back of the property.

I was surprised to find that the locks were modern, and I opened them without much fuss. I didn't feel brave enough to step out on the veranda; instead, I stood in the hallway breathing in the fresh but humid air and examining the forgotten gardens below. It was a dismal sight.

Forlorn rows of shrubby trees, half-hidden statues and a few small dilapidated buildings dotted the landscape. It looked less hopeful than the house. Large magnolia trees spilled white blossoms all over the ground and obscured what appeared to be a large sundial. *Not good planning there*, I thought. A massive wisteria vine crawled over whatever it could find, covering camellias with cascades of purple flowers and thick, brown vines. Was that a grave or a stump? I looked closer, keeping my sneakered feet safely in the hallway. Clustered in the center of the main yard was an abandoned rose garden with scrawny bushes and clumsy limbs. Despite the sound of a nearby car horn and the hum of the generator below, I felt very lonely standing on the second floor of Seven Sisters. A thick aroma of decay rolled up from the gardens, an unsettling fragrance of rotten leaves and wood. This was certainly not the pleasant view that the young woman in my dream had enjoyed. In her time, smooth lawns, flowering hedges and white-painted benches and lattice filled the landscape. It was disappointing that what was once elegant and ordered was now overrun and lost beneath a solid layer of chaos. Sadness washed over me. I couldn't help but think of Muncie, so young and hopeful despite his bleak reality.

With a sigh, I turned my attention to the stacks of boxes and plastic tubs that lined the walls and filled some of the rooms. Walking from room to room, I could see it was a work in progress, but TD and his crew were obviously talented. I loved the colors they had chosen. One of the bedrooms, the one closest to the left side of the stairs, was painted a vivid blue. The massive windows were surrounded with intricate wood molding, obviously new and painted a rich cream color. The floors were a dark walnut wood, and a chandelier sparkling with crystals hung from the ceiling. Of course, electrical lights instead of candles crowned the fixture. Except for allowances for modern building standards, it was as authentic as it could be.

I pulled on my cotton gloves and rifled through a few boxes. I unwrapped a fine porcelain piece, a perky bird resting on a branch. "This will look lovely on a mantelpiece," I said to myself. Wrapping it back up carefully, I put the lid back on the storage box. I rummaged around like a child at Christmas, careful not to undo the cautious work someone had done packing these precious artifacts. Each one had a story, a reason for being included in the collection. I continued my wandering until I came to a small box in a corner of a small bedroom. I had to prop the door open; it was heavy and wanted to swing closed. This was one room that had intact shutters, and there wasn't much natural light. I pulled my flashlight from my pocket and tossed the beam on the box. It was dusty and cardboard, and it didn't seem to belong with the neat plastic tubs and crates.

I pulled back the flaps and saw a box of papers. Digging through the box, I found letters from the late Mrs. Stuart to the Tennessee State Museum, inquiring after several items. I set the letters to the side and kept digging. At the bottom of the box were several leather-bound journals. I lifted one and rubbed my gloved hand across the cover. The engraving was worn away, so I couldn't read it in the low light. Suddenly, a shadow passed across the doorway.

"Hello? Hey, I'm in here!" I called out. I assumed it was Chip or maybe even Matthews. It was impossible to hear a car approach up here. I placed the book back in the box and stepped into the hallway. As I crossed the doorway, the door to another bedroom down the hall slammed shut. Surprised, I called again, "Hello?"

I took the gloves off and clutched the flashlight, then tried to walk quietly (and bravely) to the closed door. The creaking floorboards gave me away. I stopped at a loud creak and said a little more quietly, "Chip? Mr. Matthews?" Nobody answered, but I could hear the shifting of furniture and the soft jangling of music from behind the closed door. I took a deep breath and walked quickly to the door, turning the knob with force. It wouldn't budge. "Chip? TD?" I asked as I fought with the knob and tapped on the door. The music stopped, and suddenly the knob turned easily.

The room was bright and sunny but cool, cooler than the rest of the house. It was completely empty. I stood in the center of the room and spun around; there were no other doors except for the way I came in. "Okay, Carrie Jo, get real. It was a draft, or a crooked door that decided to swing closed." I breathed deeply and realized I was squeezing the flashlight furiously. I tucked it in my pocket, unable to fight the fear that crept up my spine. I felt the urge to leave, and quickly. I walked around the boxes, kicking a music box that was lying on the floor. The toy issued a few complaining strains and quit. I picked it up and turned it over in my hands. *Okay*, I thought, trying to calm my mind, *I must have left this out because I was just in here.* But I knew I had never seen it before. I set it on a nearby plastic storage tub and left, walking straight downstairs. I was happy to hear voices—voices of the living—in the foyer.

The incident upstairs shook me. I steered clear of the area for the rest of the day and worked on prepping some room layouts instead. By the end of the afternoon, I remembered the box with the leather-bound journals and (like a miserable coward) sent Chip upstairs to retrieve it for me. I declared it too heavy for me to carry and asked him to bring it to my makeshift office. He complied, happy to help with something besides computer work. He delivered it with a smile, obviously not chased by ghouls and goblins. On an impulse, I took a journal from the box and decided to take it home with me. I was curious to read it but more than ready to go home.

Later, I took a walk and snacked on the stuffed fried shrimp po' boy I'd bought. As I walked, I felt a tinge of sadness. I had hoped that Mobile would be a new start for me. No dreams, no screams and no one to peer at me. I tried to shake off the feeling of regret, sure I was being too dramatic because I was tired. Certainly I had imagined half of what I thought I'd seen, right? I climbed the stairs to my apartment and waved at Bette (who seemed to witness all my arrivals and departures). On the porch was a box with my name on it. It was wrapped with shiny red paper and had a gold "Emogene's" sticker taped to the front. A card lay on top, with my name printed in large, scrawling letters. I picked up my package and went inside, thankful that I was able to shut the door behind me for the day. I slid the elegant card out of the crisp envelope. A whisper of expensive cologne told me who it was from before I read the card. The card read: "Good luck on the new project. I know Seven Sisters is in good hands." Instead of signing his name, Ashland had written a big, elaborate "A." I opened the box to find a bouquet of exquisite flowers including Indian pinks, Irises and sweet tea roses. I breathed in the fragrances with a smile, locking the door and tossing my purse on the desk. I looked for a vase and found an empty Mason jar in the kitchenette. I filled it with water (still smiling) and slid the bouquet in. It was a thoughtful gesture, and I tried not to read too much into it, but it was the first time in my whole life that I had received flowers from a man. I set them on my nightstand and headed for the shower.

I needed to wash away the fear and anxiety. "I was the right woman for this job," I told myself, wishing I felt as confident as I sounded. "Ugh, I hope I know what I'm doing." As I slipped on my nightgown, I did feel a little better. I turned on the radio and listened to music until I began to feel sleepy. That was sooner than I expected even though the room was getting warm. I flipped off the radio and stretched out, feeling frustrated in more ways than one, kicking away the comforter. I slept probably a half hour, but I tossed and turned frequently and woke with snippets of dreams rolling around in my head. Some were my own, some were just memories, and there were others still that I wasn't sure about.

Restful sleep eluded me. My cozy room was too humid and warm tonight. I flipped off the window air conditioning unit. It wasn't blowing cool air at all. I opened the windows, but the warm air hung like a wet blanket. I had a long, hot summer ahead of me in Mobile. Sleeping in a flimsy nightgown had not cooled me down. Maybe ice water would do the trick; I padded to the kitchenette to get a glass. On my way back to my hot bed, I picked up the book I had left on the desk when I came in. It felt cool in my hand. I rubbed the edge of the worn book, knowing I should wear gloves but unable to bear it in this heat. I flipped on the bedside lamp and sat on the bed. Reading by the dull moonlight that streamed in from the porch was impossible. Although some of the ink had faded, the writing was intact, with delicate letters. I could see the author's name penned in the upper right corner of the first page. The journal belonged to Calpurnia!

She was long gone now, like Muncie. I pulled the sleek brochure out of the folder that Hollis Matthews had sent me. This was her! She was Calpurnia Cottonwood, the girl on the cover. I looked at the picture closely under the lamp. It was certainly her. I would recognize those almond-shaped brown eyes anywhere. They had an innocent downward slant, making her appear even more youthful than she was. In the photo, which was obviously of an oil painting, her back was turned to the artist. She looked back with a slight smile. She held a book, but the print was too small to read. I studied the girl's face, amazed that I had seen it warm and alive, flushed under the attention at a candlelit dinner party. The photo was a near likeness, a shadow of the nervous girl who struggled under the weight of an intricate hairstyle, voluminous skirts and (I suspected) the heaviness of life. I tucked the photo back into the folder, like she was a hidden treasure. "Calpurnia," I whispered into the hot Alabama night. I wanted to devour the book, read it page by page, but I was suddenly very tired. Perhaps the humidity and heat had stolen my energy.

I remembered the oscillating electric fan in a nearby closet and placed it near my bed. I set it on high and pointed it in my direction. After pouring myself another glass of ice water, I went to bed with the book. Soon the fan had cooled me down, and I began to feel sleepy. I had no idea that in my hand was a key. A key that would take me back in time again, back to Seven Sisters, back to Calpurnia and Muncie. As I closed my eyes, I felt myself drifting to a different time and place. I did not feel afraid. Perhaps I should have.

Chapter 8

My face shone strangely in the mirror, like a disembodied head, floating in the amber light of my bedroom. I hated the coiled hair piled upon my head. I looked like Medusa, the disgusting Gorgon doomed to life without love; my braids like forbidding snakes, keeping everyone away. This is what Mother wanted. I stuck my tongue out at myself, screwing up my face in an ugly look, in a defiant protest against the universe. Of course, I was not defying Mother. I'd never defy her. She was the one who had insisted on this debutante charade.

"Calpurnia, every young lady sits for a painting at your age. You'll thank me someday. Why, you're in the rose of your youth, and you're so lovely." Mother had cradled my chin lovingly, speaking softly down to me as I sat pouting on the edge of my lace-covered bed.

Compared to my mother, I felt like an old spinster, although I was sixteen—well, almost sixteen. Mother was petite with delicate hands that she kept folded in her lap when she reclined. She had smooth, dark blond hair, lively brown eyes and a tiny mouth that wore a permanent smile, without an excess show of even, white teeth. Even now, with her swollen belly and red cheeks, Mother was the picture of feminine perfection. My figure, on the other hand, maintained its childlike shape, straight like a hickory branch with no curve at all.

Downstairs, waiting impatiently in the ladies' parlor, was the insipid Reginald Ball, aspiring artist and some sort of distant cousin on my father's side. Except for his limited enthusiasm for art, he was a bore with vacuous eyes who never wondered about anything beyond the arrival of the next plate of sweets. Still, I felt a tinge of sympathy for the rotund Mr. Ball. He would always be what he was now—the bumbling son of an elegant gentleman who made no secret of his disappointment in his progeny. At least Reginald Ball had given up his feeble attempts at courting me; now we observed an easy quiet during our sketching sessions. I was quite the better artist than he but was too much of my mother's daughter to tell him so.

In the beginning, before I met him, I had secretly hoped that I would like him, maybe even love him. But that was not to be. "Strange," I told Muncie later, "artists typically have an overabundance of joie de vivre. They're searchers of the beauty in the world around them, full of artistic curiosity." I suspected that Mr. Ball's sole interest in art was merely to make a living. Had he been full of turmoil or offered even a single controversial thought, I could have overlooked his swelling stomach, round face and piggish black eyes. Reginald Ball had truly been an intellectual and romantic disappointment.

After the convening of the first sketching, my hopeful mother closed ranks on me, discreetly asking for details of our conversation. (Heaven knows why she bothered to ask since Hooney, her servant, had sat watching over us the entire time.) The dark-skinned woman had absently plucked at the threads of the small pillow she was working on, presumably for the new baby, quietly clucking at me when I'd behaved rudely or indifferently toward the boring Mr. Ball. Exasperated, I told Mother,

"He's a dreadful bore, and he licks his fingers after he eats."

My aloof father, during a rare moment of felicity toward me, had paid for the portrait in advance so that I might have all the advantages of my less wealthy but more socially skilled neighbors. Safely married and out of the way for the son he hoped he would finally have, I assumed. He brushed his sunburnt lips against my forehead after he bestowed his unwanted gift on me. I was careful not to make any gesture of unkindness toward him or to refuse him. I had sealed my heart off from my father many years ago. He was a cruel man who liked drinking corn whiskey, the spirits the slaves drink, and then lashed anything that got in his way, even Mother and me if we were unfortunate enough to cross his path.

If he had always been cruel, my heart would not struggle so, and it would be easy to keep him out. But I remember a different father. One who held my little brother with tears as he left us for heaven; a father who used to bring me soft rabbits for pets and trinkets from his trips to New Orleans. I don't remember the day that kind man disappeared, but it happened many years ago. That man was long gone. Happily, he rarely stayed at Seven Sisters, preferring traveling his properties; he said it was to manage our many businesses. He came home long enough to make my mother cry and to walk the pathways of the garden with his purposeful, no-nonsense stride. Then he was off again, leaving Mother and me the run of the house and the property for however long his latest trip would take him.

In the past two months, I had endured day-long sittings with the painter. As a quiet protest, I took particular delight in tormenting him by making slight modifications to my attire before each sitting. Changing my hairstyle or the silk coral dress with the fitted bodice and ribbon sleeves was out of the question with my observant mother. However, I did manage to make small changes, like exchanging my coral pendant on the gold chain for the jade choker or sliding a flower behind my ear. The awkward Mr. Ball spent a good half hour at the beginning of each sitting, fussing over his sketches before deciding how to best correct them. The results were predictable. Dead set on proving himself worthy of his subject, he behaved like a gentleman, never scolding me or acknowledging the changes openly. The game became boring over time. In matters of mediocrity and passivity, Mr. Ball had proven a winner.

Today, in honor of our last sitting, I wore the ivory combs with the painted roses in my hair—a gift I had received in the post a few days ago along with a note promising that by tomorrow evening, my favorite uncle would be here, at Seven Sisters! Along with the package arrived an assortment of trunks and boxes, much more than my Uncle would need during his stay. I suspected the trunks held gifts, perhaps mementos of his many adventures. Or maybe they belonged to an exciting guest.

Uncle Louis would be with us by dinner tomorrow and would stay with us for the rest of the summer. Perhaps this is why my father had decided to tour our land; he frequently and quite loudly denounced Uncle Louis, his wife's brother, as a proud man with more money than brains. Mother and Father had shouted loudly at one another before he had left again, this time taking only Early with him. I hated my father's petty jealousy over Uncle Louis. Tall with an elegant, pale radiance, my uncle towered over my father. He adored speaking French and frequently sent Mother and me books of poetry and collections of stories that we both relished. I had not laid eyes on my fair uncle for well more than two years. He was so busy traveling, acquiring new things, seeing new places. Oh, how I longed to leave with him, to see the world beyond the red dirt roads that encircled Seven Sisters—roads to my prison! I thought often that I would die here, finally stuffed inside the stone crypt along with my dead siblings. A quiet voice from deep within my heart promised that this would not be my fate.

With my chin lifted in faux confidence, I entered the parlor with a firm smile that I hoped masked my insecurity. Mother was in bed, where she would stay until the baby arrived—it was left to me to be the lady of the house to any guests, invited or otherwise. So far, I had received a local merchant, who had insisted on showing the "lady of the house" his latest collection of furniture samples, wooden miniatures that he insisted would be custom-made. How privately amused I had been when the rude fellow had managed to gain access to a mere sixteen-year-old girl with no authority to even purchase supplies for the pantry.

I also sat through an uninteresting tea with the birdlike Lennie Ree Meadows and her giggling niece. If they had held any disappointment at being entertained by me, they had hidden it very well. They were more interested in the condition of my mother and the whereabouts of my father than me. Feeling unusually generous toward our chatty neighbors, I dismissed their queries with benign and vague answers but rewarded (or distracted) the quivering Ms. Meadows with my happy news— Uncle Louis was on his way.

"Only just last week, we received the wonderful news that dear Uncle Louis is coming for a visit. He will stay for a few months before returning north to see his oldest sister, Mrs. Olivia Grant. We will be honoring him with a late spring banquet, and of course, you and your niece must come." As expected, this was the tidbit of gossip Ms. Meadows required. She quickly departed, presumably to boast that she had received a personal invitation to dinner at Seven Sisters. She would be the one to announce to the community that the elegant Louis Beaumont would once again pay a visit to Mobile. He was getting older but was undoubtedly still one of Alabama's most eligible bachelors. I giggled to myself thinking of my Uncle Louis married to the nervous Lennie Meadows.

Reginald Ball was, as I expected, pacing nervously waiting for me in the parlor, sweaty hands dipping into the sweet tray. If he had bothered to look at my hands rather than my nonexistent bosom, he would have noticed my permanently stained fingertips. Traces of my constant scribbling, as my mother describes it. "Mr. Ball," I said, smiling at him and stretching out my hand in an unfamiliar movement that I copied from my mother. "I do hope I haven't..."

Before I could continue, I met the eyes of the most beautiful man I had ever seen. He rose from one of the blue velvet chairs that faced the empty fireplace. He had a thick mop of dark, wavy hair that he wore slightly longer than the current style. He had dark blue eyes that were fringed with curled black lashes. His tanned skin was clear and warm-looking; I felt myself blush but managed a tense smile.

The stranger was half a foot taller than Mr. Ball, who was no short figure. Although his clothing clearly belonged to a gentleman, he appeared dusty and disheveled.

Mr. Ball cleared his throat. "Miss Cottonwood, I took the liberty of bringing this gentleman here, to Seven Sisters, as I found him in dire distress on the road. He says he was set upon by bandits, right on the road north of your home. We couldn't find his horse or belongings. I do hope you can assist him. I'd like you to meet, oh dear, I haven't collected your name, sir." The painter's face reddened at his oversight.

"Mademoiselle, sir, let me introduce myself. I am Captain David Garrett, at your service." He had a deep voice and a friendly manner.

We three stood looking at one another for a few seconds before I realized that I must take control of the situation. "Sir, you are most welcome here. If I may ask, how did this happen to you, Captain?"

"Blayliss and I decided to hunt for some rabbits this morning. Blayliss is a bit of a puppy but with a fine pedigree. The rabbit ran across the road in front of us, and we followed him. I rounded the curve, the one near that copse of trees, then two men stepped out onto the road. We exchanged greetings, and suddenly one of the men reached for my saddle. I began to ride on, but the two overpowered me." He paused here, no doubt feeling embarrassed. I said nothing, and he continued.

"The next thing I remember, I woke along the road with this good man standing over me. What would I have done if Mr. Ball had not found me?"

Hearing his part in the story, Mr. Ball practically glowed under the praise. "My dear sir, I venture to say you'd have found help here at Seven Sisters. However, it was my pleasure to help you in your time of need."

"Yes, indeed. Thank you, Mr. Ball." I smiled.

He turned to me. "May I thank your father or mother for your kind attention?"

"Neither is available to receive your gratitude at this time, but I will happily convey it to them. At present, my maid will show you to a room where you can change your shirt; she'll repair that tear in your shirt for you." I paused a minute before adding, "We would be happy to have you stay for dinner, sir. I'm sure by then the sheriff or perhaps my father will wish to speak to you."

"I am in your debt." His voice was low, quiet, almost intimate. But he made no inappropriate movement and did not leer at me. His perfectly masculine face was the picture of sincerity. With a nod, praying that I walked away without tripping over my ridiculously formal gown. I didn't look back but imagined the captain watching me as I left. I was pleased that I did not trip and also remembered my manners. I stopped to extend the invitation to my other guest, whom I had been warned not to forget. "Mr. Ball, of course, you must join us for lunch I think we must cancel our appointment for today, though. This is a very disturbing matter. I'm sure you understand." He nodded and giddily accepted my invitation.

My mind couldn't keep up with my heart. I barely remembered talking to Hooney and climbing the wooden stairs to my bedroom. I called out for Hannah, who sat in the hall outside my mother's door. I raced into my room and began to tug impatiently at the silk ribbons of my gown. My face looked pinker in the mirror, and I couldn't help but smile at myself. I felt the butterflies cavorting in my stomach. This was a new experience for me, and I wasn't sure how I felt about it. I stepped out of the coral silk dress and into the blue cotton gown with the purple stitching at the sleeves. It had tiny purple flowers stitched along the top of the bodice. It was my favorite gown. I had been saving it for Uncle Louis, but I felt pretty in it. I sat down at the vanity table and helped Hannah unwind the braid. "Are you sure, Miss? I like this braid on you. You look like a real lady."

Determined, I took the brush and pulled it through my hair, working out the braids carefully. "Yes, thank you." I pulled the top of my hair back away from my face and slid it into a barrette at the back of my head. I attached a blue bow and fluffed it with my fingers. Suddenly, I agreed with Hannah. I looked like a child now.

I traveled down the hall to see my mother, stepping lightly in case she was sleeping. I tapped lightly on her door before opening it. Sitting in the roomy, padded chair next to her sunny window, Mother put her book aside and welcomed me with her outstretched hands. "Well, why are you not dressed in your gown?" she asked quizzically. For the next few minutes, she listened, nodding and widening her eyes occasionally until all the events of the morning had come tumbling out.

Instead of sharing my excitement, my mother sighed heavily, her hands folded perfectly in her lap. Suddenly, I wished that I were a child again, that I could lay my head in that lap and feel her cool hands stroke my hair. "Of course, we'll have to tell Mr. Cottonwood. He needs to know these roads are not safe. We don't want anything to happen to Uncle Louis or any of our neighbors. Ask Stokes to come see me. Keep Muncie near you, would you?"

I hated that the peace of our home would be disturbed, as it always was with my father's arrival. I hated more knowing that, somehow, I had caused this disturbance. I felt guilty for feeling happy just a few moments ago.

"Now then, don't sulk, Callie. All is well. You have guests to attend to now, so off you go. Ask Hooney to set out the blue and white china and bring in some of the spring fruits. It's not every day we get the opportunity to entertain a Captain. And do be kind to Mr. Ball."

There was no sense in arguing with her or saying anything more. She was already reaching for her note paper. Before I joined the gentlemen downstairs, I visited my private library in the corner of my room and looked for a book. Obviously, anything written by Augusta Evans was inappropriate to share with mixed company. I finally selected Tennyson's Locksley Hall. I had nothing else really to talk about other than my books. I was no singer, and I had kept my love for drawing a secret from Mr. Ball, as a kindness. Sliding the book into the pocket of my blue dress, I walked slowly, as dignified as I could, down the winding stairs. My guests had made themselves at home on the porch where I had left them, and thankfully, our dinner waited for us.

In the distance, someone plucked on a fiddle. Pink azaleas lined the porch, which was cluttered with silky white camellias. We sat intimately at a round table set for three, positioned under a gnarly oak that bent graciously over us, protecting us from the beaming sun. Mr. Ball talked effervescently, snacking on sugared donuts, a generous slice of ham and a bowl of strawberries. Mobile had a new mayor, a Mr. Charles Langdon of Southington, Connecticut. Many Mobilians of Mr. Ball's acquaintance, namely his influential father, apparently had strong objections to the new mayor, which no doubt stemmed from his northern lineage. Still, he was a direct descendant of a notable hero who had fought in the Revolutionary War. I pretended to be interested as well as I could.

I pushed a strawberry around Mother's blue and white china and tried not to stare at Captain Garrett like a wide-eyed calf. I noticed he wore his own shirt; perhaps my father's wasn't a good fit for him. He was considerably larger than my father. I flushed thinking of David Garrett's arms. How would they feel wrapped around my waist? My mother was right—I was a silly girl.

Taking advantage of a break in Mr. Ball's oration, I took the opportunity to engage Captain Garrett in conversation. "Tell me, Captain, do you travel to Mobile often?"

Mr. Ball slurped on his lemonade and said, "Yes, we do want to hear about your travels. The Delta Queen, that's the name of your boat, correct?" His short dark hair stuck out above his ears, and his bald spot shone in the sun.

"I have been to Mobile many times, Miss Cottonwood. It is a city I have come to appreciate recently," he said with a smile. "I have thought many times that if I were to ever take leave of my boat, I would happily call this fair city home. How much more so now that I have found such fair and pleasant company?" He lifted his glass and tilted his head to both Mr. Ball and me.

"Ma'am, the sheriff is here to see you." Stokes stood officiously in the doorway.

"Thank you, Stokes. Just one moment, please, gentlemen." The men rose as I left the table.

A tall, lanky man with a bushy black mustache stood in my foyer. After a few pleasantries, I led the sheriff to the porch, poured him a glass of cold water and sat quietly as he interviewed our guest. He drilled through the formalities, writing down a few notes as Captain Garrett recounted this morning's misfortune. Satisfied with the interview, the sheriff mentioned that the captain's horse, a dappled gray, had been found already. The thieves must have gotten cold feet and left the horse after realizing what a shameful act they had committed. "Still, we're taking this very seriously. I have a few ideas about who these troublemakers are, but I can't be certain without more investigation. I'll do some checking around, Miss Cottonwood. In the meantime, if anyone sees the men again, please send for me immediately. Don't take them on yourself, although I can see that you're hardly alone here." I could sense that the sheriff didn't seem to approve of me. "Is your father expected to return soon?" I nodded dumbly. "Well, that's a good thing. Can't be too careful. Now, if you'll excuse me, I'd like to continue my search." As he rose with his hat in his hand, he added, "Sir, will you be available if I have more questions?"

"I am at your service, Sheriff." The captain rose to his feet and nodded slightly.

"Where can I find you? Will you be staying long at Seven Sisters?"

"No. Now that my horse has been found, I'll return to the Delta Queen before nightfall. You can find me there; I will be in Mobile for another month. I am scheduled to pick up a load of supplies and then head up the river."

"Mr. Ball, if I may have a word with you, sir," With a nod, the sheriff left with Mr. Ball, who was now fully sweating after his meal. I was relieved to see the sheriff go but felt immensely embarrassed by how my new guest had been treated.

"Miss Cottonwood, I apologize for all the trouble I've caused you. I should take my leave before you are further inconvenienced."

"Not at all, sir. I have enjoyed your company. I'm afraid Mr. Ball and I have little to talk about," I said honestly.

He laughed softly. "I can well imagine that."

I smoothed the skirt of my dress as I stood, my hand rubbing over the book in my pocket. I removed it and held it nervously. Books had always comforted me.

He smiled faintly. "Ah, Tennyson... Locksley Hall? 'When I dipt into the future, far as the human eye could see; saw the vision of the world and all the wonder that would be." He spoke the words exactly as I had read them.

"Yes! You know Tennyson?" I held my breath.

"Well, there's not much else to do on a ship but read," he teased me.

"I would love to see your ship—I mean the Delta Queen. Maybe when my mother feels better, we can take a ride. Or when I get old enough, I can go myself. We rarely travel anymore, but my Uncle Louis, Louis Beaumont, frequently travels all around the world. I guess travel is in my blood, for I want to see everything!"

He stopped and looked at me. "Don't be in such a hurry to leave home, Miss Cottonwood. It's much safer to have an adventure in the pages of your book. Many scoundrels await inexperienced travelers, especially ones as lovely as you."

"Are you a scoundrel, Captain Garrett?" I asked.

He blanched slightly. "I suspect that the sheriff thinks so, and Mr. Ball likely does by now as well. Do you think I am a scoundrel, Miss Cottonwood?"

"If my maid reports missing silverware, I shall know that you are, sir!" He laughed heartily, so I did as well.

"You have a keen wit, Miss Cottonwood." I acknowledged his comment with a nod, just as I had seen Mother do, but I kept quiet.

Later that evening, I enjoyed a quiet dinner and watched my mother sleep before I scurried back to my bedroom to record this momentous day in my journal. My candles burned brightly into the night, and I ignored the cramping of my hands. I wanted to remember everything, every word, every gesture. I even mentioned Mr. Ball in the history.

I opened my bedroom window; the smell of gardenia filled my room in just a few minutes. Pale moonlight splashed on the walls, and I tossed and turned on my bed, thoughts of Captain Garrett filling my head and burning my heart. With tired eyes and numb fingers, I eventually slept, only to dream of my new friend riding his ship across a sparkling sea.

In my dream, I saw myself standing on the shore, watching the ship sail out of sight. And then, I saw Reginald Ball, walking on the water like Holy Jesu and waving a handkerchief furiously at me.

Startled, I woke and found my father standing at the foot of my bed. Even in the moonlight, I could see he was drunk, swaying under the power of his beloved corn whiskey. Like an angry demon, he cracked his belt at my legs while he grabbed and twisted my foot. I refused to scream. I did not want to satisfy his lust for terrorizing me, nor did I wish for my mother to be his victim. She would certainly try to come to my rescue, as I always tried to help her. The belt stung my leg through the thin cotton of my gown. He sweated and sputtered, calling me vile names and hurling accusations at me. I gathered from his violent diatribe that he had had a visit from the sheriff. I couldn't prevent the tears from filling my eyes, but I still didn't cry out. How many times before had I faced this blind fury that was once the father I loved?

He raised his hand over and over again, unleashing his fury on me. My gown ripped, and I could feel the blood rise to the surface. Suddenly, something welled up inside me, something different, a wild defiance, a strange rebellion. I didn't want to die; I didn't want to be punished. I wanted to live! Blindly, I kicked at him and landed a blow right in his slim belly. With the help of the whiskey, he toppled over, falling onto a wooden chair with a crack. He howled like one of his beloved dogs, but I raced from the room. I left him, running in the darkness down the stairs. Now sobbing, I ran out of the house, into the Moonlight Garden. I scampered through the familiar maze of marble statues almost to the back fence. I cowered under a tree, my legs tucked underneath me, carefully hiding myself from the revealing moonlight.

I cried and rocked back and forth, listening intently for any intruders into my garden.

Only one came. Muncie. He said nothing but climbed in under the tree with me. He put his arm around my shoulder and pulled me close to him. I cried until he tapped my shoulder. We heard the dogs barking and sounds from the house, but no one came. I was glad he didn't try to talk to me, except for when we prayed to the Virgin for protection. We stayed there until it was nearly morning; then we crept to the kitchen house where Hooney waited for me. She clucked at my wounds and said, "Child, child." She patted the raw, red stripes on my leg with a cloth dabbed with foul-smelling liniment. Unable to stifle my cry, I released a scream and welcomed the stars that clouded my vision...

Chapter 9

I was rudely awakened by the sounds of rapid-fire knocking at my door. "Hello? CJ, I know you're in there! Come on, girl. Open up!" I rolled over in a tangle of sheets that stuck to my sweaty body. Pushing a handful of curls out of my eyes, I peered at the clock. 7:15!

"Carrie Jo! Open the door, hon!" Once again I was forced to leave my dream world behind, plunged into the reality of today. I peeked through the thin lace curtain to see Mia standing on tiptoe, looking back at me on my small upstairs porch. She had replaced her Egyptian bob with a short shock of blond hair. I was surprised that she wasn't wearing her trademark black and white clothing. Instead, her curvy body was covered in a short, red and white polka-dot sundress. Her pale skin gave her an ethereal look, but her eyes, large and darkly luminous, were completely earthly and emotional. If I didn't know her voice so well, I would have never recognized her. Only Mia could so completely transform herself in just a few months.

That was one of the things I loved about her. She had an ability to become whatever she wanted and didn't appear to feel any pressure at all to conform to anyone else's idea of who she should be.

"Coming!" I shouted at the door. Except for some mysterious new tattoos on her arm, Mia looked like a cast member from a retro '50s television show, down to her red slippers.

I opened the door and welcomed her excited embrace. She hugged me, kissed my cheek and invited herself into my muggy apartment. She chattered away about the flight and about me not responding to emails. Finally she looked at me with her perfectly lined eyes and said, "You're not ready! Get ready! We have to go. I can't wait to see this house."

I stepped into the restroom for a quick shower, leaving the door ajar so we could talk. I hopped into the shower and waited for the water to warm while Mia came and sat on the floor. She talked away as I soaped and showered. I only half-listened. I wanted to linger over my dream, but I was forced to push it to the back of my mind. I didn't feel anxious this time; I knew that I would remember every detail, probably for the rest of my life.

I hated the idea of going to work with wet hair. It didn't seem professional, but time was not on my side and I had sweated through the night. I couldn't endure spending the day smelling sweaty hair, and what if anyone got close? Ashland came to mind, and I tried not to let my mind linger on his warm hands, his strong arms or his cologne.

Mia finally came to a stopping point in her monologue about her recent travels, which I would usually find fascinating. I was able to ask her a few questions. "So when did you get in?"

"Yesterday—I just told you that! I knew you were pretty busy, being the boss and all." She was kidding, but her tone irked me a little. "Alright, now. Don't start." I reached for the loofah. "Where are you staying?"

"Oh, you know me. I'm couch-surfing. I'll always be an anthropologist. I've got to check out the locals." I heard her rummaging in my medicine cabinet.

"Mia, are you sure that's safe? Do you know this person? Whose couch are you on? Where exactly are you staying?"

"Not far from here. I walked it, actually. Down off Royal Street. My host works at a nightclub down there, but he has fabulous reviews on the surfing site."

"Is that really a good idea?" I wasn't really surprised by anything Mia said or did. She was definitely her own person. She always had been since I'd known her. I simultaneously worried about and admired her.

"Oh, yeah, my host is pretty legit—and interesting. He works at Gabriella's. It's very exclusive, and it's beautiful inside. They completely restored the building. Love that brick."

"You've been inside?" I tried not to sound shocked.

"Stop worrying, Mom. Besides, Henri Devecheaux is absolutely fascinating, and he's very spiritual. He also looks great in a dress!" She laughed wickedly.

"Well, if you change your mind..." There was an awkward silence, and then came the question I was expecting.

"Hey, have you talked to William in the past few days?"

I wanted to ignore the question but felt obligated to explain myself since it was Mia who had introduced us. I had thought that at one time William and Mia could have made a go of it. They had spent a lot of time working together, huddling together on a private project, but apparently it was just work. I turned the oversize shower handles slowly, stalling for time. I reached my hand out for a towel, and Mia obliged.

"I've been meaning to call him, but I never do. I guess I don't know what to say. I mean, what we had was nice. He was nice… I just don't know. Something is just not quite what I need it to be." I squeezed the water from my hair and wrapped my body in the pink, fluffy towel. I pulled back the curtain slowly. "I really like him, but on so many levels we…"

"Oh my God! What happened?" Mia's dark eyes were fixed on my right foot.

I followed her gaze to a massive bruise on my right ankle. My tan skin was blue and purple and seriously swollen. Nausea swept over me, and I sat clumsily on the commode. I stared at the wounded area, then pulled up my towel to check for more bruising. I half expected to see welt marks along my legs. I stared at Mia. "I don't know…" I couldn't process what I was seeing.

"Don't give me that. There's no way you could not know. Look! It's obvious that these are fingerprint bruises. Who's been manhandling you? Was it William?" Mia's dark eyes flashed angrily.

"No! Never, he'd never. I don't really know…" I could feel swollen tears filling my eyes. I didn't want to believe that a "ghost" from the past could actually reach me, touch me.

"Does it hurt?" She lifted my foot and examined it carefully.

I pressed on the skin. "It's a little sore, but that's it."

"You want to tell me what's really going on here?" Mia looked into my eyes, laser-like.

I sighed. "Sure. But this may take a while. Let me get dressed. We'll grab some breakfast, and I'll tell you what's happened."

She nodded, and I left her to get dressed. I opted for some purple jeans and a casual red top. I wound my wet hair up on top of my head in a perky bun and took a minute to tap my lashes with mascara and dab on peach lip gloss. I scribbled a note for Bette, asking her to check out the air conditioner, and left it on her door. Thankfully, she wasn't home this morning. I would hate to refuse her company. I was relieved that she hadn't gone to the trouble of making those biscuits she had promised me.

We rode in silence to the Golden Egg, a tiny breakfast shop I had spotted on my drive into Mobile. Sliding into the vinyl-covered booth, I felt calmer, even hungry. We ordered some bacon and eggs and thanked our young waitress for the basket of biscuits and butter she cheerfully deposited on our table. Mia sat looking at me expectantly.

"I don't know what to say," I muttered with a shrug.

"Don't be shy around me. You know I'm jealous. I don't think you're crazy—just tell me! How many dreams have you had here?" She leaned forward.

I took a deep breath. "Here's how it started." I told her about my embarrassing fall my first night at Seven Sisters and about Muncie.

She broke in, "Well, that's it! That's how you got the bruises."

"Shh…" I looked around, embarrassed. "That's not it. Besides, that's the wrong foot—and there's more." Her eyes widened as I told her what I saw in my second dream; about the soft-voiced Calpurnia, the handsome yet suspicious Captain Garrett and of course, the cruel, larger-than-life Jeremiah Cottonwood. I was not surprised to see Mia pull a small notebook out of her purse and jot down some notes as I talked. When it was all over, she looked at me with her mouth open.

"Carrie Jo, this is amazing. All of this is simply amazing. Are you okay, though?" She paused, looking at me carefully, "Are you really sure you are okay? We could call Dr. O'Neal," she finished in a whisper.

"I'm perfectly fine. I just can't believe this is happening. These dreams are different than the ones I've had before. I can actually feel what she feels, what he feels. I know what they're thinking. I could smell the wisteria, taste the lemonade and see the clouds sailing by. I know it really does sound, well, crazy but it's like I'm them." My voice shook, but I was determined not to burst into tears in the middle of the Golden Egg.

Mia didn't say anything—she just watched me. Finally, she leaned back against the cracked vinyl seat and tilted her head. "Do you know how lucky you are? What I wouldn't give to experience just a few minutes of seeing the past, of being there? I love the past. I love history. You are a real dream catcher. The real thing, and you don't even see it."

I looked at my plate that I had barely touched, surprised at the scolding. The over-easy egg had congealed; the once creamy grits were stiff and unmovable. I felt a shift in the air. The uneasy "invisible" moved around me, and I shivered. I stared back at my friend and said, "Lucky? Is that what you think?"

I could feel her anger rising. "I just mean you have something that other people wish they had. It's not a curse, CJ. It's a gift," she said matter-of-factly and leaned forward to touch my hand. I couldn't help but pull away.

"Pardon me if I don't share your perspective. Where have you been the past ten years, Mia? You of all people know how weird I am, how different. You would really want to live like this? Afraid to lay your head down and close your eyes in a strange place?" I felt aggravated and a little mean. "I don't think you'd be doing much couch-surfing."

Her perfect red lips curled up in a rueful smile. "Ouch, okay. I'm sorry." She reached across the table once more with her manicured hand and tapped mine. "Tell you what, I'll tap into some resources and see what I can find on your cast of characters. I'll help you find answers, CJ. You aren't alone." With a squeeze of my hand, all was forgiven, at least on her side. And for Mia, I guess that was really all that mattered. Her indifference stung.

Before I could respond, she gasped, "Look at the time! It's 8:30!"

"Oh, Lord," I said as I scrambled out of the booth and threw some cash on the table. We didn't say much as we drove to Seven Sisters, and the silence continued when we pulled into the long drive.

"Wow," I heard her whisper.

"Uh-huh," I agreed.

Looking quite like a butler in his black dress pants, vest and white shirt, Matthews met us at the door. "This must be Miss Reed," he said jovially. He extended his hand to Mia, and the two chatted for a moment while I slipped past them. I took a moment to stop by the ladies' parlor. It was bare now, with only the makeshift desk, two dusty chairs and the reclining sofa. It was all wrong and missing so many details. I walked to the door that led to the porch and discovered that the old door wouldn't budge. Still, I could see the wilderness that was once a garden through the dirty window. I pushed aside the sadness and instead quietly pledged to make it right…whatever "it" was. "I will make it right," I whispered into the air.

"Hey, daydreamer," Mia teased, "Come show me the setup, then take me on a tour."

I laughed, my sadness forgotten. I left the stuffy room behind and took Mia on a tour of the house. We finished in the Blue Room, where we had installed the computers.

I found Chip, our IT guy, hunkered over his computer. He had short, curly hair, which made his ears appear even larger than they were. He gave me the usual nonchalant wave but perked up and sat a little straighter in his chair when Mia strolled in behind me with her red fingernails, retro ballet flats and vintage dress. I made introductions and listened to them chatter about the new program that he had designed for our "little" project. He clearly knew what he was doing; although he was no history major, the young man had more than adequate knowledge about networking, firewalls and password control. We'd be working with some expensive antiques, some that had been delicately restored. It was so important that nothing came up missing. Butterflies flipped in my stomach, reminding me that I would be the one responsible for anything that went wrong. Still, for a few minutes, I felt sane and happy and completely in control.

Ashland walked in with perfect timing. I was beaming from ear to ear, and he gave me an equally brilliant smile. He wore an untucked blue linen shirt with jeans. He looked comfortable and sophisticated, even with his tanned arms full of boxes.

"Oh, here, let me help you with that," I said with a laugh.

He looked as if he wanted to say something but instead looked past me. I turned to see Mia standing there, looking a schoolgirl holding a notebook and pencil to her chest.

Before I could say anything, Ashland spoke. "You must be Mia. I recognize your face, even though your bio picture looks very different. Can't change those eyes." He gave her a half smile and extended his hand for a shake.

She took his hand slowly and rubbed her pencil eraser against her lip. I felt uncomfortable, mostly for Ashland. With a grin and a low voice, she said, "I am Mia. I suppose you are the Master of this Plantation, Ashland Stuart?"

"I'm not anyone's master, but I am the boss."

Mia playfully slid on top of a nearby desk and tapped it with her fingers. "So, boss, is this where you want me?" I couldn't believe my ears or eyes, and I felt my face flush bright red. I had seen her use the direct approach before, but never on a client or someone she barely knew.

I jumped in. "Um, over here, Mia. This is your spot, I believe. Right, Chip?" Changing the subject and hopefully the trajectory of the conversation, I asked, "Chip, is the wireless printer online yet?"

"Should be, but let me print a test page just to be sure. If you and Mia could do the same from your computers, that would help."

I nodded, too embarrassed to look at Ashland until he tapped me on the shoulder. "Got a minute?"

"Sure, I can spare a few minutes. What's up?" I spun around in my chair to face him.

"I want to show you something, but you'll need to put your tennis shoes on. Did you bring them?"

I nodded and went to my desk for my gym bag. I pulled on some socks and my Nikes and was ready to go.

I repositioned my ponytail on the way out of the Blue Room, purposefully avoiding Mia's stare. *What just happened? Did Mia think Ashland would be won with a little awkward flirting?* He was certainly not her type. Usually, Mia's guys were quirky—sometimes handsome, sometimes plain, but always quirky. There was nothing quirky about Ashland Stuart.

He didn't mention Mia's show or what he thought about her, and I was too professional to bring it up. "Have everything you need? For the office?" he asked. "Matthews promises me that you do, but if you need something else, please let me know."

"Certainly, I will. I think, so far, we're doing all right. I expect this place will be like a beehive for the next few months with remodeling the house and setting up the museum."

"Yes, it will be, but that's the fun of the whole process. You know, I minored in history in college. I love the history of Mobile, but there is so much we don't know. I feel honored that I get the opportunity to help others remember it like it should be remembered." I didn't know what to say, so I just nodded.

"I have something to show you. I hope you're feeling better. How's that bump?"

"Great! Thanks again for your help. I can't believe how clumsy I was."

"As long as you're okay."

I felt a surge of happiness knowing that he cared. In the back of my mind, I heard Calpurnia's question: "Are you a scoundrel, Captain Garrett?"

Ashland continued, "I want to show you an interesting discovery. It takes a little walking, but it's nice out. And I think we'll have a clear path getting there. They've cut back some of the underbrush already. This find is truly amazing. TD found it this morning. That's why I was late."

He had certainly piqued my curiosity. "What is it?"

"You'll see, but wait; do you have your phone?"

I patted my back pocket to make sure. "Yes, of course!"

"You're going to need it." He laughed.

"How mysterious."

We jumped off the back porch; the steps were soft and spongy, too hazardous to use. I was happy that I didn't embarrass myself and fall in front of him—again.

"It's a ways ahead, past this small section, into the…"

"Moonlight Garden…" I blurted out.

"Yes, the Moonlight Garden. How did you know about that?" He paused on the pathway, looking like a Greek statue standing in a wild, green garden.

"I must have read about it someplace. I mean, I am a researcher." My excuse sounded weak. I knew about it because I had already been here, along with Calpurnia and Muncie, cowering under a sculpted fir tree. I had seen the two friends huddled in the wet rain, fearfully praying.

"Not many know about the garden. Even I'm not sure about the actual layout, and I own it. Still, it's not common knowledge that it's called the Moonlight Garden. Do you happen to know why it has that name?"

I felt my cheeks redden again. I wondered how much I should tell him, from what I had heard in Calpurnia's mind in my dream. How she had subconsciously named the statues as she wove through the complex arrangement of hedges and trees. The Moonlight Garden was a maze, with seven landmarks, statues of the demi-goddesses of the Pleiades or the Seven Sisters. They were Sterope, Merope, Electra, Maia, Taygete, Celaeno and Alcyone. Their parents, Atlas and Pleione, stood in the center. I decided not to tell him these details; how could I explain that? Instead, I said, "The statues of the garden were made of white marble that reflected the moon. During a perfectly full moon, the statues shone bright, like a Moonlight Garden. It's not as mysterious as you think."

"You seem to know a lot about it. I'm glad I hired such a good researcher." He led the way to the beginning of the maze. It wasn't nearly as beautiful as it had been, but I was happy to see that some of the important spots remained—a tree here and certain flowers there. I caught my breath just realizing how much I could remember.

"Well, I'm not psychic. I promise you that," I said, a bit tongue-in-cheek.

"What do you mean by that?" He stopped and looked at me sharply.

I couldn't understand it, but I knew that I had made him angry. The joy of the day drained away under the stare of his blue eyes. "It was a joke." I laughed nervously. "You know, that I'm not a psychic telling you these things. I'm just an average researcher."

His jaw popped a little. "It's not far ahead, just beyond the first two clumps of trees there."

For the second time that day, I had to ask myself, *What just happened?*

We walked a few more minutes, and I managed to avoid most of the sticker-filled dewberry patches but chided myself for not giving my skin a good douse of bug repellent before setting off on this journey. I tried not to be irritated by Ashland's unpredictable moods. He swung his machete at some branches and ignored me. And I returned the favor. I made myself a thousand promises to keep him out of my mind, although it was tough not to watch his muscles ripple under his blue linen shirt. But I silently pledged to speak as little as possible to him until we entered the clearing.

We stopped in a small clearing, and under a copse of oaks and pines stood a forgotten mausoleum with the name "Cottonwood" etched above the door. It was made entirely of hewn stone blocks that fitted together masterfully. The mausoleum doors were green, evidence of copper, with a huge keyed lock below the right door handle. It had a peaked stone roof that looked intact, down to the window grates. It stood about eight feet high and was large enough to hold a large family.

Large tears welled up in my eyes. I thought of Calpurnia's hopeful face, how she imagined a life in the world beyond her privileged prison. I wondered if she managed to escape, and if she did, was it to another pretty jail nearby? I slid my sunglasses down, over my eyes, quickly dabbing away the wetness.

"And there's more. We found a dozen small crosses over here, but there's nothing written on them. There's really no telling who else is here."

"This is pretty amazing. Let me grab my phone." I began snapping pictures and emailing them to myself so I could examine them later on my computer. I couldn't believe TD had found this.

"I wonder who we have here. I mean, obviously, someone in the Cottonwood family, but who? I suppose there are some records somewhere?" He seemed genuinely curious about who lay at rest on his property, and I couldn't blame him. I shuddered to think that Jeremiah Cottonwood may have been lying just a few feet away from me. The wound on my ankle twinged.

"Hmm…that should be easy to find out. I imagine Mr. Cottonwood and his wife and perhaps their children.

What was the daughter's name? Calpurnia?" I snapped away with my phone, pretending I didn't know. I was not a skilled liar. I squatted next to the small white crosses, hoping my question didn't give me away.

"No, it couldn't be her. Probably her parents, though." His large hands touched the stone crevices, feeling where they met so perfectly.

Genuinely curious, I asked, "Why couldn't it be? Did she get married and move away?"

"No. She went missing—sometime in the 1850s, I believe." I felt like someone kicked me in the gut, but Ashland didn't seem to notice. He continued, "It was a serious scandal for the time. They looked for her for years, even made some accusations, but no one was ever arrested. Lots of people have tried to discover her whereabouts; even my mother was obsessed with finding her. It consumed her life her last few years. I'm sure she often thought of her when she came out here."

I heard the sadness in his voice; this obviously touched him deeply. "It is a riveting story," I said. "Young heiress goes missing. She must have been something of a celebrity in her time."

He nodded. "I expect she was. And Miss Cottonwood wasn't just wealthy; she was extremely wealthy, the heir of two fortunes, the daughter of two established families."

Although standing in the woods with Ashland was many a girl's dream come true, all I could think of was getting back to the apartment to pore over the first journal, Calpurnia's journal. I had to know what happened to her. We stood looking at the mausoleum and the crosses. Except for the buzzing of mosquitos, all was quiet. "Thank you for sharing this with me, Ashland. This is an amazing find. I'll have to come back with a decent camera."

He wiped the sweat off his forehead with his hand. "You're welcome. We'd better get back. As hot as it is, it will probably rain soon."

As we trekked back to the house, my mind raced through the possibilities. I now had two missions: find both Muncie and Calpurnia. Where could she be? My mind naturally went to the most likely suspect, her father. I knew his brutality firsthand.

"Did you hear me?" Ashland asked.

"I'm sorry. No, I didn't. What did you say?"

He sighed a little. "I asked you to dinner."

I shrugged. "Sure, but I'm not much of a cook if it's potluck."

He laughed out loud. "What? Why would I ask you to dinner and ask you to cook?"

My eyes widened. "Oh, dinner...so, not for everyone...just me and you? I thought you...um..."

Ashland chuckled. "Wow, I feel like I'm in high school here. Listen, Carrie Jo, don't feel compelled to say yes because you work for me. And contrary to what you might think, I'm not usually this forward."

I felt my brow furrow. "I don't think anything at all. You just caught me off guard a little—I guess I was daydreaming. I would like that, but I have to do something first. Can I get back to you?" I smiled at him.

"Okay...are you seeing someone?" Ashland looked anxious, but I didn't want to explain that I needed to "break up" with William. Even though William and I had kissed just once, I felt like I owed him some honesty, if nothing else. Carrie Jo Jardine was not the kind of girl to two-time.

"No, it's not like that. Can I get back to you?" With that, we finally made it to the back door.

"Sure." He gave me a nod and didn't stay long after that—I hoped I hadn't scared him off.

Mia greeted me with, "Gee, you guys were gone for an hour," apparently forgetting her earlier theatrics with Ashland. Of course, I couldn't wait to show her the pictures. Her eyes lit up. "Ooh...that is so cool. Okay, I'm wearing jeans tomorrow, and you have to promise to take me out there. You know what, let me do some checking. I bet we can find out who's buried there."

I rubbed the sweat off my forehead with a paper towel. "What do you think about the little crosses? Children? Pets?"

"Probably children, but we may never know without digging them up. Hey, before I forget, don't make plans for tonight. I've got a surprise for you later." Mia pressed her red lips into a smug smile.

I chuckled. "Oh, Lord, I'm worried about what that could mean. Sure that sounds great." I was happy to think we could get our friendship back on track.

By the end of the workday, we had assigned furniture to three of the rooms downstairs, deciding that the Augusta Evans book collection would be perfect for the ladies' parlor. The men's parlor would house rare pipes and a small collection of pistols from before the Civil War. The future Seven Sisters Museum was beginning to take shape. It was a good feeling to see that, to be a part of the restoration. The following week, I would be meeting with someone from Mobile's African-American Museum. Ashland had made it clear that he wanted this important facet of antebellum life highlighted. We would have access to some photographs and artifacts, which I planned to distribute throughout the house and the other buildings that were to be reconstructed here.

* * *

Just a few hours later, Mia and I were walking down nearby Dauphin Street. Flickering gas lamps welcomed us into a candlelit restaurant called Bevere's. I loved everything about it, especially the high ceilings and proper linens. After some back-and-forth on what to order, I had to ask, "Mia, what happened today?"

She looked up from her shrimp cocktail. "What are you talking about?"

"I'm talking about what happened with Ashland. The whole 'You're the boss' thing. He doesn't seem like your type at all."

Her face was blank, and she said in a low voice, "He's Ashland Stuart. He's everyone's type. He's also the handsomest guy I've met in a very long time. Not to mention he's uber-rich. And what does that mean? 'He's not my type.' In case you haven't noticed, I don't have a type."

"I'm sorry, Mia. I didn't mean to embarrass you or hurt your feelings. I was just wondering."

She popped a shrimp in her mouth and chewed. "No worries, doll. I gave it a try, and it didn't work out. No biggie. Hurry up and eat, though. We have to be at our destination by 8 p.m. I know it's a Thursday night, and I promise not to keep you out too long."

We chit-chatted a little after that. I asked about her parents, and she confessed that she hadn't seen them in over six months. I missed them; I had spent a lot of time at their house during college. Thirty minutes later, we were standing in line at Grand Central Station, a bustling nightclub, waiting for a spot at the bar. It was hopping, even on a weeknight. Two spots together finally came open, and we slid onto vinyl-covered stools. Before I could ask what was happening, the lights dimmed, and a spotlight hit the stage.

It was William.

Chapter 10

The audience clapped and cheered, but I couldn't move. This certainly had been a day of surprises. William sat on a wooden stool in the center of the stage and pulled the mic close. He strummed his guitar and played "The Heart of Love," his most popular song. He had a brilliant smile that he used often, along with a perfect voice. And in just a few verses, the audience was in love. You could see it. Unfortunately, I wasn't. He was my friend but nothing else, no matter how badly he wanted to be—or Mia wanted him to be. I didn't understand why she was so invested in my relationship with him. I could feel her give me a sidelong look, but I refused to look at her.

The second song into his set, William spotted us at the bar. I gave him a weak smile, and Mia waved. He had the audience swaying in their chairs, especially the ladies, and why not? His shoulder-length dark hair and green eyes captivated many of them. Once his performance ended, William worked his way to the bar, stopping to talk to some enthusiastic fans along the way.

"Mia! Why didn't you tell me?" I whispered to her. This wasn't how I wanted to do this, face to face.

"I thought you'd like it."

"Hey! What did you think?" William hugged Mia and then me.

"You were brilliant, William. They love you, and we do too. Right, CJ?"

He smiled even more broadly, and I offered, "I love the new song, the one at the end."

"Thanks!"

After an awkward silence, I asked, "So, when did you get in?"

"I was going to call and let you know, but then Mia said we should make it a surprise. I got in last night, and I'm booked for the next two weeks. Maybe longer, if the Mobile crowd likes me. How's the house? When do I get a tour?"

Mia had headed to the dance floor, no doubt leaving the barstool for William.

"Listen, William, can we talk? You know, outside? It's kind of loud in here."

With a sigh, he agreed, and we walked out of Grand Central and down the brick sidewalk. To the casual observer, we might have looked like a loving couple, me in my summer dress, William looking smart in his crisp gray shirt and black dress pants. I couldn't remember seeing him dressed up before. "You look nice. I don't think I've ever seen you wearing something besides jeans."

"Well, whose fault is that?" A playful grin spread across his face and then quickly disappeared. "Uh-oh, you don't look too happy, CJ. What's up? I have a feeling I already know."

I stopped and just blurted it out. "William, you are a wonderful man, and I think of you as a friend, but..." I took a deep breath, "I can't say that I feel anything except friendship toward you. I hope that you didn't come all this way because of me. I am sorry."

William's green eyes flashed, and he looked like I had slapped him in the face. "You think I came down here for you?"

I sputtered, "I just assumed that you..."

"I told you months ago that I was sending some demos out. Thanks for listening. Look, I get that you don't like me like that, but I think I'll live." William had taken a step away from me. I'd never seen him angry with me before. "Listen, I have to go—the next set is starting soon. Let's just..." He raised his hands in the air and then turned and walked away, leaving me alone on the sidewalk in downtown Mobile at night.

Pausing for just a moment, I decided to walk home. Humiliation and confusion rose like waves inside me. Riding back with Mia wasn't a good idea right now, and she had coerced me to leave my car at home. The only other people I knew in town were Ashland, Bette and Matthews. It didn't seem appropriate to call any of them.

Eventually, anger fueled my stride. I didn't think much about walking by myself until I reached the end of the street. Dauphin Street had been busy and well-lit, but the surrounding side streets were lined with oaks that kept them shadowy. Discreetly, I slid my hand in my purse and felt for my phone just in case I needed it. But really, what was I going to do with a cell phone? Other than a catcall from a passing car and the occasional fellow pedestrian, nothing happened. I climbed the stairs to my apartment and unlocked the door. I was met with a blast of cool air. The new air conditioning unit was working beautifully.

My phone dinged—a message from Mia, but I didn't bother opening it. My heart said something was wrong, but I couldn't put my finger on it. Instead of checking in with my old "friend," I typed in Ashland's cell number and sent him a message with shaking fingers. It simply said, "How is your weekend looking?" with a smiley face. Not a minute later, he texted me back, "Great! Dinner tomorrow night?" I tapped in, "Sounds great. 7pm okay?" I got a smiley face back. "Oh, Lord, what am I doing?" I groaned as I threw the phone on the bed. "Am I actually going to date the boss?"

It was still early for me, and I couldn't go to sleep without investigating the journal I had smuggled from work. I kicked off my shoes, slid into my pajamas and snuggled into the soft cushioned chair next to my bed. It was deep and perfect for curling up in a ball. I flipped on the lamp and took the book in my hands. I examined it cover to cover. It was a leather-bound journal with an engraved monogram in the center. The letters were faded—might have been a "C" or maybe even an "O" or a "G," but I knew whose it was. I opened the cover and confirmed it: *Miss Calpurnia Christine Cottonwood.*

She had a neat, slanted penmanship. The faded letters looked light brown and were almost gone in other places. I thought about putting on my gloves, but I wanted to feel the book, feel connected to her. With a deep breath, I opened the book and walked into her world...

Chapter 11

April 20, 1850

Dear Diary,

Mrs. White had her puppies all over the bottom step of the staircase. I suspect she was trying to carry herself up the spiral staircase to my room but the climb was simply too much for her and her enormous belly. I am Thankful that it was Hooney who found the scattered litter and not my father or someone else who may have been tempted to drown them in the river. I am happy to report that the new family is safely ensconced in my armoire. What a sight to see all those precious, white faces in my old hatbox! I expect they will call the space home for a while, at least for a month or so.

Today, I prayed in earnest that Mother's baby would arrive soon. I'm loath to name the baby "sister" or "brother," as I hear from the slaves that this is bad luck. I prayed extra last night to break any curses I may have spoken over it in the past. How wonderfully entertaining it will be to have a sweet-smelling baby to sing to and share my stories with! (Hooney snickered at me and said, "Babies is a lot of things, but sweet-smelling ain't one of them." I rolled my eyes at her and got censured by Mother.) Honestly, the True and Genuine Reason for my prayer was for Mother. This will be her fourth try at having a son and Heir for my father, with thus far no fair results except for me. As I am surely to marry soon to whomever pleases my father's fancy, an heir will certainly be needed, and no girl either. Mr. Cottonwood wants a strong, strapping son to take the reins of Seven Sisters, not a disappointing, spinster daughter. So I pray and hope for only the best news that Mother will safely deliver a boy and that I will marry in the Fullness of Time; however, I am careful not to speak that aloud.

Dear Cousin Isla is a great comfort to me. She has a great wit and knows more dances than I and is a far better singer. She says things that make me blush and scolds the new upstairs house girl constantly. I do reprimand her, but sometimes I wish I could be more like her, free and unencumbered by worry and duty. She told me her father has been long dead but her mother is my own Mother's dear sister. I have never had the occasion to meet Aunt Olivia, but I'm sure that, like Isla, she is a great beauty. It is a boon to have someone to talk with, and I will forever be in Uncle Louis' debt for bringing her to me. How often of late I have poured my heart out to her. How comforting to be assured that all will be well, that a husband, handsome and charming, will be found for me, even if I am tall, flat-chested and not musical in the least. We have pledged to marry close kin so we could be near to one another for the rest of our lives.

I had hoped to spend time with Uncle Louis today, but again he's been riding with Father. They are taking a survey of the land, the improvements to the riverfront and the extended quarters for the slaves. I have barely seen my uncle on this trip, but he assures me we shall continue our conversation as soon as possible.

Mr. Ball came to give his regards to my cousin but could not be compelled to stay for lunch, strange as that may seem. I wondered that he did not, as I've never known him to pass by a plate or bowl without dipping his hand in it. I suspected that he may have had intentions to court my cousin, but as she had no one to whom he could present his request formally, he simply dithered about without saying much of anything before excusing himself. I suspect he will return at a later time. Isla says she would rather be thrown off the top of Seven Sisters than be courted by or married to Reginald Ball. I had to laugh, but of course I did scold her for such a foolish notion.

April 21, 1850

Dear Diary,

What a blissful, delightful day! This morning, I received three calling cards, one belonging to Captain David Garrett! How happy I am! Although I was not able to formally greet my guest, Cousin Isla assures me that he asked after my health and well-being multiple times. And since he "Could not speak to the lady himself," he chose to write me a note...

> *Miss Cottonwood,*
>
> *It pleases me to thank you once again for your kindness toward me during my hour of need. Truly I have not seen such great hospitality as the cordiality I received at Seven Sisters. I feel ashamed that you had to rescue me and that I was not rescuing you, dear lady. I pray that we shall meet again and soon so that I may properly show my gratitude toward you and your family.*
>
> *Your faithful friend,*
>
> *David Garrett, Captain*

Words cannot express the joy I felt receiving this note from the Captain. How I nearly fainted when I read it! Cousin Isla assures me that he trembled while he wrote, hoping to convey his deepest thanks without offending in an unseemly manner. She told me that she encouraged him to speak honestly, to confess his true heart in the matter. Although his written message was succinct, Cousin Isla assures me of the deep levels of sincerity he displayed. I feel sure that somehow, some way, I shall see the Captain again and give him my equally solicitous esteem. I took the liberty of returning his note with my own:

Dear Captain Garrett,

Thank you for your kind words. You are most welcome for the care that we provided you. I encourage you to make yourself available to my father, Mr. Jeremiah Cottonwood, at your convenience, sir, so that we may talk further.

Kind regards,

C. Cottonwood

How I labored over the note! I tuck it inside my gown every day, hoping for the opportunity to present it to my new friend, with all discretion, of course.

April 25, 1850

Dear Diary,

How can I describe to you the utter depths of my misery? All the joy of life has left us as the search continues for dear Uncle Louis. All of his effects remain carefully stored in his rooms, but alas, we have no word of his whereabouts since these many days past. What an event it had been, Father and Uncle Louis participating in loud and raucous debate, one that echoed through the house and even up the staircase. I had seen the horses ride up the dusty lane but thought nothing of it when another left shortly after. There was always a commotion when menfolk are about, and plenty had been around for days, except for Captain Garrett.

To listen more closely, I decided to peek out my door and found my mother swaying at the top of the stairs, looking as pale as a beaten sheet. "Mother, why are you standing here?" I said. "Come, dearest, you should not be here in the draft." I looked down to see her gowns stained red, and blood also dotted the carpeted floor. Her bleeding had come, and no one was to be found! I screamed to see the blood, so much blood. And in a flash, Hooney came upstairs to see what was amiss. She said something in a language I did not understand and ordered me to help her get Mother back to her bedchamber. I caught Muncie peering up the stairs, concerned for me, I'm sure, but I waved him back. Since he was a "man" now, my Father said, "He has no place on the top floor, and I'll whip the hide off him if he comes back." I believed him.

As much as we tried to coax her, Mother would not speak to us but only stared off into space, like someone who was locked in a dream. I cried, "Mother, Mother, what is wrong?" I patted her hands, rubbing them furiously, but she didn't see me. "Now, look," Hooney said to me in a stern voice, "You go down them stairs and tell Stokes to send for the doctor. He should never have left the other day—and then go tell your Father—or better still, your Uncle Louis—that Mrs. Cottonwood is in a bad way. Send one of them girls up here too—I need some clean clothes and water. Now, go on! Get going, Miss!" I did what I was told and scurried down the stairs like a madwoman. Unable to find Uncle Louis in the parlor or the Blue Room, I sprinted to my Father's study and told him the urgent news. He set down his whiskey glass and rushed passed me, looking like a ghost, his face drawn with concern and confusion. How I felt for him in that moment! I could not find Stokes, and I noticed that Early, my father's constant companion and slave, was also missing. But I did find Muncie, who nodded and left right away to request the doctor's presence. Dear Muncie!

That was many days ago, and I am sad to report that the baby quickly passed from this life on into heaven, where my other siblings waited for her with a pair of wings. At least that is what the priest told me. Another daughter, another disappointment for my father. I had not been present when she slid into this world, I imagine in a pool of deathly blood, but I had dreamed of a baby crying in the night. I was supremely surprised to learn that it had indeed been a dream, as the sound was very life-like to me. Mother was still not speaking; Hooney says she only grunted a little when the baby, I will call her Angelique, came forth. There would be no funeral for baby Angelique, only a quiet sliding of the stone door and a quick deposit of a tiny bundle of forgotten life on a cold slab.

To bring further sorrow, Uncle Louis remains gone from Seven Sisters. The Sheriff rummaged through all of his accoutrements, papers and personal effects but found no clue of where my Uncle may have ventured. Isla and I have been inconsolable, crying and praying constantly for his safe return.

I pray all day and night that my Mother will return to me. I miss her gentle hands and bright conversation. All our happy days together are too few, and I plead constantly with God to give us more. Why would she be in such a state? What horrible thing did she see or imagine that frightened her, down to her soul?

Oh, Diary, what shall happen to us all?

I wiped fat tears from my eyes, careful not to stain the delicate pages. I read the passages over and over again. There was more—much more—but I needed time to process all that I had learned. I looked at the clock; it was close to midnight. I uncurled in the round chair, slid the journal into a manila envelope and replaced it in my bag. I flipped off the light and slid into my cool sheets, thankful again for my kind landlord. It took me a long time to fall asleep, and when I did, I could swear I heard a baby cry.

Chapter 12

My day began with an impromptu breakfast with Bette in her comfy kitchen. My thoughtful landlady had prepared us praline-pecan French toast with fresh fruit and sausage patties. I have to admit that until I met Bette, I wasn't much of a breakfast girl. But she definitely made me a believer. I was glad I was starting the day so pleasantly, since I knew I had some unpleasant things ahead of me. At least I had a date with Ashland to look forward to and, of course, all of Seven Sisters to explore. Calpurnia was on my mind heavily; it was so tempting to spend all night diving into that journal, but I had to keep life balanced. It was dangerous to think about the past so much that it took up all my present. I had learned that lesson the hard way.

"Thank you for fixing the air conditioning. The new unit is working like a charm, and I slept great last night."

Bette smiled at me warmly through perfectly applied lipstick. She had a soft, ivory complexion and even whiter teeth. She was attractive, and I imagined she had been striking in her prime. "That's no problem, no problem at all. This isn't the old days. We can't sleep without air conditioning in Mobile. I don't know if it's gotten hotter or if we're just spoiled now. I remember when the only AC around here was at the library. I sure spent quite a few summers reading ridiculous love stories when I was young." She wasted no time serving me generous helpings of everything. "I know you have to get going soon, but I'm just dying to know how the restoration is coming along. My sisters and I, at the

Historical Society, that is, are all atwitter about the commotion. I heard the grounds are looking better and better."

I nodded, unable to resist digging my fork into the fluffy French toast. "I wish I could give you the inside scoop on the remodeling, but Matthews has made it pretty clear that I have to keep quiet about the details." I felt genuinely sad about keeping all the excitement to myself, but I couldn't break the confidentiality clause in my contract.

She patted my hands; hers was soft and cool. "I don't want you to get into trouble. That Hollis Matthews is a strange bird, isn't he? Okay, okay, I'll tell the ladies they will just have to wait." She sipped on her coffee. I loved her coffee cups, fine white china with a gold rim. I appreciated that she brought out the good dishes for me.

Maybe I was just missing having a friend to talk to, but I felt like I could trust Bette. I blurted out, "I can tell you something, though, something we found that wasn't in the house..." I whispered, "We found the old Cottonwood mausoleum."

She set her cup and saucer down with a clink. "No...oh my goodness. That is something, isn't it? I bet it was hidden under all those vines and bushes right there on the property. There's no telling what you will find on that land." Her hand flew to her chest. "Oh, I wish I could see it!"

I remembered the pictures on my phone, so I dug it out of my purse and tapped the screen. "Here. I have a few pictures right here." I did not think it wrong to share with her the details I knew about the cemetery—that was public knowledge. Besides, I hoped that Bette might know something about Calpurnia, so I had to ask. "Ashland was telling me about that missing heiress, Calpurnia—the one who disappeared before the Civil War. Have you ever heard of her?"

Bette dug a pair of reading glasses out of a nearby drawer and was peering at the pictures attentively. She looked at me with wide eyes. "Oh, yes, most everyone in Mobile knows about her. But I imagine Ashland could tell you all about that. His mother was obsessed with finding Calpurnia Cottonwood. The late Mrs. Stuart was a very intelligent woman, something of a scholar before she married Mr. Stuart. But in the end, it became a kind of obsession with her. Some people say that the Cottonwood girl ran off with a military man. But I don't know, they didn't really do that sort of thing in those days. Others say that one of the slaves probably killed her and buried her on the plantation."

Bette looked up from the phone and put one arm of her glasses in her mouth, trying to drum up a forgotten thought. "Now, I've also heard that old Mr. Cottonwood did her in when he was drunk. That man, by all accounts, never passed up the chance to tilt a bottle. And he gambled his wife's money away...well, much of it, anyway. But that was so long ago, it's hard to know what the truth is and what is simply plain old rumors. You know what they say, 'Nothing makes a Southern story better than a stretch of time and a few glasses of gin.'" Bette pursed her lips and shook her head; her curls bounced around her face. She handed me back my phone, too polite to ask for copies of the pictures. I was thankful, as I'd have had to say no.

I asked, "Tell me about Mrs. Stuart. What was she like, and why did she become so obsessed with Miss Cottonwood's fate?"

"Emily was her name, Ashland's mother. She was from a very fine family from the northern part of the county. Remember? She was a Hunter, and later she discovered the Hunters were a part of the Beaumonts, one of Mobile's oldest families." After dropping that bomb on me, Bette kept talking. "Emily was tall and athletic; she beat me more than once in tennis, but she was very much a lady. I remember when she first got married— oh, she was the talk of Mobile. So lovely in that big old chiffon gown. You know, back in the '60s, it wasn't a wedding gown if it didn't have umpteen ruffles."

I nudged the conversation along. I would circle back to the Beaumont comment in a minute or two. I didn't want to be rude. "You say you two played tennis together?" I poured more syrup on my French toast; I wasn't really hungry any longer, but I desperately wanted this conversation to continue.

"Our husbands were members of the same country club; we played doubles a few times. His name was Gerald. I wasn't crazy about Mr. Gerald Stuart—he liked to talk over her too much. Sometimes I would ask her a question, about her son or something else, and he'd answer for her. That drove me crazy! She did love that boy, though. He was her everything."

I took a sip of my coffee and ignored the clock. It was getting late, but the conversation was riveting. "So is Ashland an only child?"

"Yes. I think she wanted to have more—she did love children, but he was the only one. When her husband died, I half thought she'd marry again. Mr. Stuart had a cousin that she seemed especially fond of—handsome man, can't remember his name, but nothing happened. However, Mr. Stuart left her an extremely wealthy woman, as well he should have, as unkind as he was at times. Drive through Mobile, and you'll see the Stuart name all over the place."

My phone dinged. I glanced at it and saw Terrence Dale's name pop up. I hit the ignore button.

Bette didn't let my interrupting phone stop her story. "When she bought Seven Sisters, we thought for sure she'd restore that place, but she didn't. I hate to speak ill of the dead, but I think the poor thing kind of lost her marbles. All that money and that sweet boy, and she spent all her time trying to find that girl who was long dead."

"When you say Beaumont, you mean that Emily Stuart née Hunter was a descendant of the Beaumonts. As in the family of Christine Beaumont, who married Jeremiah Cottonwood?"

"The very one!" She looked supremely delighted to be the one to tell me this news. "That means that Ashland is also related to the Cottonwoods." She smiled, rose from her chair and started picking up plates and dishes.

I jumped in to help, wanting her to continue but not wanting to push.

"Oh, thank you," she said. "I'm sorry I'm dithering on. You'll have to excuse me. I'm just so excited that the big old house is going to get the treatment it needs."

"I'm happy to listen. It's nice to hear what the local community thinks and what stories you can share with me." I added warm water and soap to the sink. "I'll wash these while you put the food away. I don't know where anything goes."

"Thank you! I didn't invite you over to wash the dishes, but obviously you were taught manners growing up."

I smiled as I washed the glasses and cups. "You say she lost her marbles. What do you mean?"

"Well, she started hanging around a different crowd, a lot of psychics and mediums and such. She even tried to get the Historical Society to sit in on one of those séance things; you know to boost the energy or some such. I told her I couldn't do that, I was a Baptist!" She laughed heartily, and I did too. "I think my friend Cynthia Dowd did, but she didn't want to talk about it. Poor Emily gave so much money to those charlatans. In the end, all the money in the world couldn't help her find that girl. Anyway, Emily got pneumonia. Poor Ashland found her in the garden, nearly dead. She died just a few days later."

I felt a surge of sympathy for Ashland to have lost both parents so young. Still, he appeared to be coping with life fairly well. He was educated, committed to restoring important historical sites in the city and, of course, independently wealthy. That was the legacy his mother left him.

"When you can, Carrie Jo, when it's allowed...will you come speak to the Society? We would love to hear from you. Maybe tell us something about the process or how you got started in the preservation field?"

"Sure, I'd be happy to. It will probably be a few weeks before I can, though." I gave her a bright smile and dried my hands off. "Looks like I'd better go; time is getting away from me." I grabbed my purse and phone and said goodbye.

I left Bette's feeling happy, having found out a little more about Ashland and Calpurnia. Did I believe a slave killed her? No, but Mr. Cottonwood was certainly a likely suspect. The Hometown Donut Shop was on the way, and I decided to stop and pick up a few pastries for the crew. We'd have at least six of us working inside the house today, not to mention all those that would work outside. A couple dozen donuts would be a nice treat. I pulled into the packed parking lot, grabbing the last spot. Fortunately, the line wasn't long. I stepped up to the counter and ordered three dozen plain donuts and two cartons of orange juice.

The little diner was bustling; even the counter was full. I surveyed the crowd and locked eyes with William. He didn't say anything to me, but he raised a foam cup as a greeting and then quickly turned his attention back to his donut. *Hmm...I guess this is how it's going to be now.* The perky server brought me my order, and I clumsily stacked up the boxes and tried to get out the door without losing any. William was on his feet in an instant, pushing the door open for me. He followed me to my car and opened the rear door. I slid the donuts in and arranged the juice cartons on the floor. "Thank you."

"I want to apologize for last night." William ran his hand through his dark hair. "I was wrong to go off on you like that. I guess, well, I guess I was really hoping for a different conversation."

"I'm sorry too. I should have had this conversation with you before I left, but to be honest, I was a coward. I like you, and I value your friendship. I wasn't fair to you."

He tucked a wisp of my hair behind my ear to stop it from whipping my face in the morning breeze. "Always worried about someone else, CJ. It's okay, I promise." As I drove away, I wiped a tear off my cheek. *I did like him only as a friend. Right?*

The crews were working outside, setting the grounds free from choking vines and gnarly underbrush. Junk trees, like old "popcorn" trees, were being cut down. But of course, no one was touching the live oaks. Rotten wooden siding was being replaced, and I could see the beginnings of Mobile's newest living museum come to life.

I waved one of the crew over and handed off two of the boxes of donuts and one carton of juice. I headed indoors with the remaining goodies, feeling confident and happy. Inside were Mia, Chip, three interns from the University of South Alabama and, of course, Matthews. Somewhere in the house, I could hear TD working on wood. Except for the finishing touches, the Blue Room and a small side room were nearly completely restored and ready for use. The rest of the house would be restored in sections, with careful attention to detail. I could see TD had placed heavy plastic over the doorway to the Blue Room, since the door had not been hung yet. That would keep dust from collecting on our equipment. I was happy to feel cool air in our room. Someone had brought in a tower AC unit. *What a brilliant idea!* I was relieved to hear the upstairs was cool as well.

Seven Sisters was a unique project compared to the few others I had worked on. Those had involved off-site planning projects, and here, we had the opportunity to work right in the environment. I would be deciding on how the home would be restored and what we would be presenting to the public. I felt the weight of that responsibility even more now that I had seen firsthand what life here had been like. I took the donuts and juice to a little table we had set up in the Blue Room. I opened the box and set out some paper cups.

Matthews was the first to arrive at the table. "Thank you, Carrie Jo."

"My pleasure. Have you heard anything from C. M. Lowell on those mantelpieces? I know it's only been a few weeks, but TD is going to need to install them before they cut the molding for the rest of the room."

"Right. I'll put a call in to them this morning. I'd forgotten about that. I've got some leads on paintings for the two main parlors. One is pretty incredible; I emailed you photos of both of them. Don't forget, we've got boxes of paintings in the attic. And good news—we have air up there now, too. If you can't find what you want, there is plenty of room in the budget, but many of the local families are willing to allow us to use their pieces. With all credits, of course." I couldn't figure Hollis Matthews out: one minute he was cold and distant, and the next he was kind and friendly. One thing I knew for sure—he was always a man with a plan.

"Great. I'll check out those pictures and let you know. I've got some plans ready for the ladies' parlor, including a significant display of Augusta Evans books. I'll have those to you by the end of next week."

With a nod of his salt-and-pepper head, he walked away, probably off to call about those mantelpieces. I invited the interns to have a donut and took a few minutes to get to know them. There were two Rachels, Rachel Kowalski and Rachel McGhee, and James Pittman. All of them were excellent archaeological students who had earned their spots on our team. I'd Skyped with them individually before I came to Mobile, but this was the first time we'd met in person.

"Well, guys, are you ready for the grand tour? It's the same one visitors will take once the museum is open." We started in the ladies' parlor, continued on to the men's parlor and the Blue Room, and then went up the opposite side of the hall to the servants' waiting area, the music room and the ballroom. There were of course a myriad of closets and smaller rooms that wouldn't be shown to the public.

Chattering like the excited teens they were, they climbed up the spiral staircase. I stood in the hallway right where I had read about Mrs. Cottonwood bleeding over a century ago. I pointed to the bedrooms on the right and the guest rooms and private sitting room on the left. We walked through the rooms, starting with Calpurnia's, then on to the three other rooms on the same side of the hall. The hairs on my arm stood up in a few places, but I shook it off. I supposed that seeing the place I'd been reading and dreaming about was giving me the shivers. There were no strains of music or slamming doors. I breathed a sigh of relief.

"Okay, let's head back down and talk about what you'll be doing." In the Blue Room, Mia was printing off material and stapling papers together. We hadn't spoken, but I gave her a small smile and thanked her as she brought me the paperwork. "Rachel K., I've got you working on the ladies' parlor. I've sent you an email about it, but let me just show you what I want." We talked for a while, and then the interns were off to work on their tasks. I turned my attention to a more challenging task—repairing my relationship with Mia.

Chapter 13

"I know what you're going to say…" Mia immediately went into stress mode. "And you're right. I never should have interfered with you and William. I guess I thought I knew what was best for you."

We stood alone in the ladies' parlor. *How appropriate*, I thought ruefully. *The place where drama has unraveled for nearly two centuries.*

"You can't do that, Mia. You can't just apologize without hearing me out. You have to listen first. That's how friendship is supposed to work." She clamped her mouth shut and nodded as I continued. "I know I was a wreck in high school and even more of a wreck in college, but you have to stop. You can't fix me. You don't get to pick who I date. Besides, it seems to me you and William would make a better couple than he and I would—did."

"Don't you think I wanted that to happen? I was crazy about William, but all he wanted to talk about was you." Mia's eyes watered, and a tear slid down her powdered cheek. "I've liked him since freshman year, but he never so much as asked me out. We hooked up once, and that was just because he got drunk at Solomon's at the Ren Wrap Party."

"Mia…" was all I could say. I touched her arm and then dug in my pocket for a tissue. "Then why on earth would you try to get us together?"

"I wanted him to be happy. I wanted you to be happy. I don't know."

She started crying, and I hugged her. "I'm sorry. I didn't know, Mi. I wish you had told me so I could be there for you."

After a minute, Mia wiped the tears away. She jutted her chin out slightly and said, "I have something to show you." That was my friend, ever changeable. But I rarely saw her emotional.

"Sure, whatcha got?" I was happy to get off this heavy subject. I sensed that there were more feelings lurking under the surface of those pretty eyes and stylish clothes, that she still wasn't happy with me, but I wasn't sure. I *was* sure she would tell me if she wanted to talk about it.

I followed her back to the Blue Room, and she waved me over to her computer. I pulled up a chair and listened as she presented her findings on the mausoleum. "Did you know that there was once a garden here called the Moonlight Garden? Well, of course you do. You dreamed about it, right?" I made a gesture for her to lower her voice. She continued in a whisper, "Anyway, the mausoleum is located due north of the center statue of the Moonlight Garden. What's interesting is the white crosses you found around the mausoleum are arranged in the exact formation of the statues in the garden."

"So the crosses aren't grave markers?" I asked, curious about the connection.

"Could be." Mia shrugged. "But what are the odds that they would be in the exact alignment of the statues? I mean, exactly like the garden statues. Look. According to this old drawing a visiting author made here sometime at the end of the 1840s, this was the location of the Atlas statue, the god who was the father of the Pleiades. Just outside the garden was Pleione, the mother who protected the family. These crosses are all markers. I blew up the photos of the crosses you sent me. Did you notice the names engraved in them? Well, partial names. Most of the letters have been worn away." Mia pointed at the screen. "See, this is Sterope. This one is Alcyone…"

I just stared at the screen. "How could I have missed that? What does it mean?" I could see the names, but I wasn't convinced that it meant anything other than that the old Cottonwood family had an appreciation for Greek mythology.

"You're the historian," she said with a laugh. "I'm the anthropologist. You can't figure that out? It's obviously some sort of map… or something."

"I don't doubt you found something significant here, but I don't see a map yet. Tell you what, you keep working on this. Maybe later this afternoon, we can walk back to the mausoleum and take pictures of all the markers. At the very least, it would make a neat tidbit to share with visitors."

"Sure, sounds great." I could tell Mia was disappointed at my lack of excitement, but I had so much to do. Getting sidetracked by a hunch wasn't something I wanted to get mired in. I patted her on the shoulder and left her to work on her research, happy that at least we had a truce of sorts. I printed the layout proposals and went in search of TD. We needed to get on the same page with our remodel priorities. I had certain ideas and plans for the opening ceremony, which was scheduled to take place in six months. We had to make sure that at least these opening exhibits were ready to go.

The handsome contractor had been working on the ground floor earlier, but I couldn't find him. I went upstairs and saw only Rachel K., who was cataloging the contents of some of the boxes in one of the guest rooms. I waved at her and walked back toward the spiral staircase to continue my search outside, but I paused in front of Calpurnia's room.

The door was ajar and swung open easily with a gentle push of my fingertip. I stepped into the empty room and stared at the bare fireplace with the missing mantelpiece. I missed the elegant furnishings, including the armoire and mirror. I walked to the window that overlooked the driveway. In Calpurnia's day, it would have given her a lovely view of the carriageway. I touched the cool painted wall. TD had chosen a light peach for this room, which was close to the original color. The room had been an even lighter shade of pink. It was small in comparison to the others on this floor, but I loved it. I touched the window and felt the urge to sit in the wide windowsill. I closed my eyes and imagined Calpurnia sitting here, looking for some sign of David Garrett or Uncle Louis traveling up the driveway to see her.

I stayed still, half hoping I could conjure up images of the past, to see without dreaming here in this room, but it didn't happen. The chainsaws in the yard and the voices of the excited interns downstairs all traveled into the room, preventing my ears from finding the quiet they needed to truly hear. Suddenly, I could hear Rachel and James talking, and the conversation was amplified as if they were in the room with me. Rachel was excited that Professor Cooper was giving her four weeks of class credit for landing a spot on the Seven Sisters Project. James bemoaned the fact that no such courtesy had been extended to him. According to his professor, it was business as usual. And as a matter of fact, he was expected to deliver a report on his work at the mansion at the end of the semester if he wanted extra credit. I left my leather portfolio on the windowsill and crawled on the floor to the nearby cast-iron grate. It was like listening in on a telephone. I pulled my phone out of my pocket and used it as a flashlight, shining it into the dark vent. Something caught the light and glinted, but I couldn't reach it with my fingers. I made a mental note to come back with a screwdriver later. It was probably just a screw from the grate, I figured.

I wondered if this phenomenon worked in all the rooms. *Rachel and James must be below me…* I wandered from room to room, checking for sound from the grates. I heard music playing from the ladies' parlor, maybe Tori Amos. Chip was talking to someone on the phone in the men's parlor; it sounded like his mother again. Poor Chip. *No wonder he was always leaving the room to talk on the phone.* I could hear Mia and Matthews having a heated discussion from the grate in the Blue Room.

"Have some patience. If what you say is true, that she's dreaming already, then there's no reason to hurry. Let's wait and see what happens." I knew that angry voice; it was Matthews. The next voice was inaudible, but I could tell that he was

talking to a woman. *"What does that matter?"* Matthews sounded aggravated. *"Who cares what he thinks? Listen, stick to the plan and stop improvising and scheming. Just do your job and keep your mouth shut. Too many people know about it already."*

"Don't think....because...I'm not one to...play with me and you'll be surprised." I was sure that was Mia's voice. My heart pounded in my chest. Somehow, some way, I was being betrayed.

"Carrie Jo, what about this?" Rachel K. was standing in the doorway, probably wondering what I was doing lying on the floor. She held up the music box that had played its strange solo the day before. "Looks like we need a key to play it. It wasn't in the box."

I got off the floor and dusted myself off. I faked a smile and took the box from her, giving it a cursory glance. "I'm not sure what to do with this stuff. Looks kind of modern. Thanks, Rachel. I'll figure it out."

"Okay. Are you all right?"

"Yes, I was just...yes, I'm fine. Thanks. Listen, don't forget to copy me on the list, okay?"

The perky intern bopped down the hall, her dark ponytail swinging. I decided to play it cool. Nobody knew that I knew anything. *Let's keep it that way. Put your game face on, Carrie Jo.*

I went back to Calpurnia's room to get my portfolio from the windowsill, but it wasn't there anymore. It was lying on the floor. The pictures had slid out of the unzipped book and now lay in an unorganized pile. I set the box down and squatted to pick up the papers, restacking them neatly.

From this angle, I could see into the vent. That was no screw from the grate—it was the key! The tiny silver key for the music box. How had it gotten in there? With a rush of emotions, I crawled to the grate and tested it by pulling on the edges. Nope, it wasn't going to budge. I felt in my pocket and found my small utility blade. I used it like a screwdriver. The screws came up more easily than I thought they would. In just a minute, I lifted the grate and reached for the tiny key. I shoved it into my pocket and replaced the grate, racing to get the screws in as I heard TD calling for me. I met him in the hallway, and we took our scheduled tour. I deposited the music box Rachel gave me on my desk and left Mia in the Blue Room without saying a word. I had a lot to think about and an endlessly growing list of mysteries to solve. To top it all off, I had a date with Ashland Stuart in just a few hours.

Like the girl from long ago who intrigued me so, I could feel the events of life swelling up around me. Destiny was unfolding its complicated pattern, and I was a mere thread in the tapestry.

Chapter 14

Ashland insisted on picking me up that night. As I carefully shampooed my hair (that bump still hurt) and later ransacked my closet for something suitable, I reviewed my trip to Mobile thus far. As it stood, I had a sore leg, a bump on my head and handprints on my ankle, and I had probably lost a good friend—no, two good friends—for an undetermined reason. One of those friends *might* also be betraying me somehow with a man I found repulsive and crafty.

On the upside, I was dreaming more clearly than ever before, I had the job I always wanted and I was going to spend some time with Ashland Stuart. I was looking forward to getting to know him better. He seemed intelligent and quick-witted, and he was of course very handsome. I suddenly regretted putting all my "date" clothes in storage in Charleston. In the end, I opted for white jeans, a blue and white striped top and navy blue flats. I looked at myself in the mirror. *Hmm...jeans aren't too snug. Okay.* I pulled my hair into a low ponytail at my left shoulder and dabbed on some makeup. *Well, he said I should dress casual, so I am!*

Ashland knocked on my door a few minutes early, but thankfully I was ready to go. As I climbed into his car, I waved goodbye to Bette.

"You look great!" He gave me an appreciative smile. I couldn't believe I was doing this, going out on a date with my boss. He was out of my league, really, but he had asked. I tried not to think about the why too much.

"Thanks. You did say casual. Where are we going?" I fastened the seat belt and put my small purse down by my feet.

"Do you like seafood?" The car slid through the tunnel that led to the causeway across Mobile Bay. "This area has some of the best. You'll never have shrimp like Gulf shrimp, I promise!"

My stomach grumbled, and I was happy to chit chat with him. "Oh yes, I love all types of seafood. Are we going to a restaurant?"

"No, I thought we could have dinner on my boat." The sun had fully set, and the stars shone brilliantly over the bay. I gasped as a meteor whizzed across the sky. "Look at that!" I squealed with delight, rolling down the window so I could see the sky better.

"See, I've even arranged for entertainment." Ashland laughed and rolled his window down too. A few more flew by—we were in a genuine meteor shower. We crossed the bay in a few minutes and pulled up to the Fairhope Marina. "I've never been on a boat before," I confessed.

"No worries. It's a big boat, and the seas don't look too rough tonight, so it should be pretty smooth. We won't go out far, just outside the bay, and then we'll have dinner. I've cooked something special for you."

"Gee, I hope you didn't go to any trouble, Ashland."

He looked at me thoughtfully. "That's nice."

"What's nice?"

"You calling me Ashland. I like that." He stepped out of the car and went to open my door. I was finding that he was a true southern gentleman. I liked *that*.

"Do you trust me?" He gave me a wide smile. *God, he's handsome!*

I nodded once, accepted his hand and stepped out of the car. I promised myself I would not trip this time. We walked down the planks to the boat, and my eyes widened. It *was* a big boat. As a matter of fact, it was the largest one in the marina, as near as I could tell. I could hear the tinkling of glasses and people laughing. Apparently lots of people had planned to watch the stars fall tonight.

I chuckled at the boat's name, "Happy Go Lucky." We stepped aboard, and Ashland gave me a tour. It had several rooms, an ample kitchen and a full-size bathroom complete with Jacuzzi tub. I felt like I was in an old episode of the Lifestyles of the Rich and Famous with Robin Leach. Well, okay, maybe not quite that luxurious, but it was close.

Ashland led me to the dinner table he had set up on the deck. I could see that he had a server waiting for us, who held out my chair and handed me a fine cloth napkin. Ashland's eyes twinkled as he opened a bottle of champagne. The server brought us covered dishes; with a flair, he removed the covers. They were plates of cold, boiled shrimp with cocktail and tartar sauce. In a few minutes, we were served West Indies Salad, stuffed flounder and cocktails.

"My compliments to the chef," I told the server. He looked from me to Ashland.

Ashland grinned. "I'm the chef."

"No! You can cook? Hidden talents. Thank you for going to the trouble of doing all this for tonight.... Oh, look; here comes some more stars..." We made a toast to the stars, and eventually neither of us could eat anymore. We washed our hands and settled down on a cushion at the bow to watch the skies. That night was the Leonid Meteor Shower. It would be ending soon, but I wanted our time together to go on and on.

Ashland sighed. "The stars are so beautiful tonight. You know, in the winter, you can see the Pleiades—the Seven Sisters—in the Northern Hemisphere. Actually, there are nine stars, but only seven can be viewed with the naked eye. They say they're dying stars and will fade away soon."

"Mia mentioned something about that to me the other day. She said she believed those white crosses we found were actually markers because they had the stars' names on them. They were pretty faded, though; I didn't even see them until she pointed them out to me. She's convinced it's a map to something." I sipped my cocktail absently, staring up at the stars.

"A map to what? Did she say?" Ashland was staring at me. I felt a surge of worry, but I wasn't sure why.

"No, she didn't. I told her those markers didn't mean anything. They could just be names of children who died at birth, or even markers for family pets. I mean, who knows, really?"

He looked serious; his jaw was clenched a little. He set his drink down on the side table. "I think it's time I told you a little about my mother and why I'm restoring the old house. You see, my mother's family were descendants of the Cottonwoods—and the Beaumonts, even though they later moved to the northern part of the county. My mother loved that old house, and she spent a lot of time there in her last years."

"Bette, my landlady, she's with the Historical Society, and she told me a little about that." I wanted to let him know he didn't need to dive into painful memories just to fill me in. I wanted to save him some heartache.

He smirked. "Well, people do talk."

"Oh, no! Bette isn't like that at all. She knew your mother, and she really liked her. She didn't say anything negative." *Except that she had lost her marbles.*

"That's good to know. You probably know that my mother was obsessed with finding the heiress, the Cottonwood girl. She did everything in her power to locate her, even hired detectives and researchers to follow the leads she uncovered. Nothing ever came to fruition. My mother's theory was that the girl was killed because of a treasure, a necklace that was worth a remarkable amount of money. Don't get me wrong; the Beaumonts and Cottonwoods were wealthy, at least before the war, but Mr. Cottonwood had made some bad investments and had done who knows what with his fortune. And he had his eye on his wife's. Mrs. Cottonwood's brother wasn't willing to see his sister's inheritance squandered by a man he hated. So, with her consent, he took her fortune out of the bank and put it all in a small collection of jewelry. She could keep her money in her own hands that way. It was the only way women back then could."

"Wow, that explains so much."

He looked like he didn't know what to make of that comment, but he continued. "According to the local historians, Mrs. Cottonwood invested the money in diamonds and sapphires. The largest piece in the collection was a necklace called The Seven Sisters. It was seven sapphires, with two diamonds, set in the swirling formation of the stars. It was quite the showpiece. She was never seen wearing it, but in her will, she left it to her only living heir, Calpurnia Cottonwood. It was my mother's theory that after Mrs. Cottonwood died, Mr. Cottonwood killed the daughter or sent her away so he could get his hands on it. At least, that was her theory."

I didn't know what to say or think for a minute. I said in a quiet voice, "Is that why I'm here? You want me to find this treasure?" I felt a keen sense of disappointment. Had I been wrong to come to Mobile? Had I been wrong to accept his dinner invitation?

"Oh, no, not at all. I'm just telling you about the 'treasure' because I felt like you needed to know. Please believe me when I tell you that I didn't hire you to find a necklace. I want to build a museum, one that helps the city and the region remember its past. I feel like I owe that to my mother, to my family. I don't want you to find the necklace, but I am asking you this: help me find out what happened to Calpurnia. I can't explain it, but I need to know."

He reached out and covered my hand with his. The stars fell around us, some skidding across the sky like quiet angels falling into the faraway sea. Others simply appeared and disappeared, leaving nothing behind but a moment of awe and brilliance. Ashland leaned toward me, one hand on mine, the other on my cheek. I closed my eyes as he kissed me. And I kissed him back. His lips were soft and warm, and I could have stayed like that forever.

As I pulled away slowly, I whispered, "Yes, I'll help you find her."

Chapter 15

We spent hours talking about the house. How we would move the flow of traffic through the home, what rooms we should include on the tour and how much parking we could accommodate. We talked about the mantelpieces that were finally delivered and when we would begin reconstruction on the kitchen house. We didn't kiss again, but we held hands and watched the stars. Eventually, I looked at my watch. "Oh my goodness, it's after midnight!"

"I'd better get you home. I had no idea it was so late. Hold on just a minute." After he left, I walked along the boat and watched the moonlight dance off the water. This had been the perfect date—stars, water and Ashland's sensual kiss. I ignored the nagging, suspicious voice that said he was just using me. That he really did want me to treasure-hunt for him. *Shut up! Is it so hard to believe he likes me?*

In a half hour, we were driving back across the causeway. Jazz played quietly on the radio. "Thank you for a lovely evening, Ashland. It was breathtaking to see those stars falling."

"The evening isn't over yet, is it?" he asked me playfully. I blushed, glad that he couldn't see me in the dark. I didn't know how to answer him.

We exited off the interstate and on to Government Street. I was taking mental notes, learning how the city was laid out. Government would take us right to my apartment. From the exit, I looked down over the city and easily spotted Seven Sisters lit up like a Christmas tree.

"Ashland? Who's working at the house tonight? TD or Hollis Matthews, maybe?"

"Nobody that I know of. Nobody's supposed to be, anyway."

"Well, someone left some lights on. Can we stop by real quick, just to check it out? We just got that shipment of Pena ceiling medallions in, and I would hate for anything to come up missing."

"Yes, we'd better." We turned on the private road, surprised to see three cars lined up in the driveway. I recognized one of them.

"What the hell?" Ashland was clearly not amused.

"Hold on, that's Mia's car. I didn't give her permission to be here. What in the world is going on?" Maybe she came to see the mausoleum in the middle of the night, but I wished she had told me she was going to be here.

It was eerily quiet, and fog was rolling up from off the river. The house sparkled with light against the murky backdrop of mist.

Before I could say anything, Ashland was on his phone. "Matthews? Call me when you get this message." He then called the police, who told him to wait for an officer to arrive.

Ashland and I looked at one another, and it was clear neither of us wanted to wait. We got out of the car and headed for the house. The path to the front door was much easier to navigate now that the azaleas had been cut back and thinned. But the sidewalk was broken in some places, and I nearly tripped over a crack. Ashland reached out to steady me and didn't let go. The satyr leered at us as we passed, his tongue poking out perpetually, mocking the unwanted visitors to his lost garden. I shivered.

"Do you hear singing?" I asked Ashland as we climbed the steps, still holding hands. He nodded but didn't say a word. I could see he was angry. I wondered if he knew who the other cars belonged to. What could they be doing here at one in the morning? Yes, someone was singing softly, a chant or something. A soft female voice whimpered and cried. It was coming from upstairs.

We stood at the bottom of the stairs, and I had a mental flash of Muncie peering up the spiral staircase and Calpurnia waving him away. "Go back," she had mouthed to him. *Is that what we should do?* With a wave, Ashland told me to follow him. We walked upstairs, unable to avoid the squeaking and complaining wood that echoed after every few steps. But nobody came out to see what the noise was.

The light at the end of the hallway was on, but the singing—no, the chanting—was coming from the first room on the right, Calpurnia's room! The wooden door hung open, and from the slit of light we could see three figures sitting on the floor of the mostly empty room. There were candles burning, and I could smell incense.

Ashland was ready to storm into the room, but I held him back for a moment. I heard a girl's voice whimper and cry, "*Mon dieu, aidez moi.*" She repeated the phrase over and over again.

Then I heard Mia's voice. "What do you need help with? Who are you?"

"*Mon dieu, aidez moi!*" The girl's voice was more intense, getting louder.

Ashland looked at me, his blue eyes dark and furious. "There's a child in there!" My eyes widened with surprise. I followed him as he pushed the door open. "What the hell is going on in here?"

A breeze blew past me, sending chills down my spine, and the candles flickered and shook. Mia sprung to her feet angrily. "Wait!" she cried out. She was with a large black man in a gray suit. I didn't know him. Unfortunately, I knew the other man with them.

"William?" I nearly shrieked. He looked away, ashamed, and I saw a tiny smile on Mia's lips.

The man in the gray suit said, "I am Henri Devecheaux. I am here at the request of Mia. I do hope that is all right. It was not my intention to break any law." His voice was deep and rich.

"Where's the child?" Ashland demanded.

Mia laughed at him. "What child? There is no child here—well, not anymore."

I stepped forward. "Who was just here? We heard a child crying." She didn't say a word and just stared at me. "Is this some sort of game, Mia?"

"This was never a game to me, Carrie Jo. Never, not for one minute. You know why I'm here. Don't pretend you don't." Her voice was calm.

"I have no idea why you're here, Mia. I never gave you permission to be here. I don't even know how you got in." Ashland watched us carefully; I supposed he was trying to figure out what was going on. So was I.

"Does your date know about your secret power? Does he know how you communicate with the dead?" Her lip curled. I couldn't believe what she was saying. "Does he know what you really are?"

"Mia! Why are you doing this?" I felt confused, angry. I wanted to strike out at her, but I didn't.

From the window, I could see police lights below. I took a deep breath. "I suggest you go downstairs and explain yourself to the police." My hand was shaking as I reached for the nearest candle and blew it out. William paused when he passed me but wouldn't look at me. Henri excused himself and apologized again, but Mia said nothing as she left us. We were left standing in the room with a few candles and some chalk drawings on the floor. I grabbed a nearby work cloth and wiped them away.

It felt wrong in here now. Not peaceful or happy, just wrong and troubled. Like Mia. What had happened to make her hate me so?

"Carrie Jo? What was she talking about? Didn't you hear a child in here?"

I knew I would have to tell him everything, and soon. I just didn't think I could do it tonight.

"I did hear a child's voice, but it was probably one of them," I explained away. "Trying to have some fun with us. They must have known we were climbing up those stairs because they squeaked so bad. I don't know what's happened with Mia." My hair stood on end. I was pretty sure we had heard the voice of a child, one who had lived here long ago, but I knew that it was not Calpurnia or Muncie.

"What was she talking about? Are you some sort of psychic?" He spit the words out; I knew how much he disliked psychics.

"No, I'm not psychic, not at all. I never asked her to do...this, whatever this is. And I promise to tell you everything, but let's talk to the police now. I need to get any keys she may have stolen and change computer passwords before we leave." I paused at the door. "I'm sorry, Ashland."

He put his hand on my shoulder and pulled me to him. We stayed like that for a moment, remembering how perfect the evening had been before all this. "You do know we have to fire her, right?"

"Let's go do it now."

The police asked us a few questions, but Ashland did not want to press any charges. He wanted to keep the incident out of the papers. I pulled Mia aside. "I don't know what kind of stunt you were trying to pull, Mia, but it has gotten you fired. I hope it was worth it."

Her dark eyes were full of emotion, but I couldn't fathom what she might be thinking. She left with William, and Henri made it a point to personally apologize to Ashland again for the intrusion. He handed me his card and left us to finish up the police report.

Once we were alone, we went from room to room, checking closets and doors. I think Ashland needed to make sure there really was no child here. I didn't need to look. It was after three now, and the stillness outside began to creep indoors. It was the sort of stillness that promised lurking danger. I don't know if I was just tired or if I was seeing things, but the shadows began to move erratically. I heard every creak in the old house. I didn't like it.

"Ashland, let's go. Will you take me home?" Fear crept over me. I had the overwhelming sense that we weren't alone in the house, that someone or something was watching us. I wanted to run away. Far, far away. I walked out on to the porch, feeling some relief. Ashland flipped off the last light and joined me.

"Well, this will be a date you'll never forget." I laughed at that but quickly walked to his car. I wanted to go home and climb into my bed. I wanted to forget Mia and William. Forget the uneasiness I was feeling.

"I know I said I would tell you everything, but it's really late—or really early, depending on how you look at it. Can we talk tomorrow? Maybe have lunch or something?" I needed to think about what I would say to him, and I was so tired that I might not make sense. This was going to sound crazy enough as it was.

"Yes, that would be great. I'm exhausted too." He started the car. "I just need to know...can I trust you?"

I looked at him squarely in his handsome face. "Yes, Ashland, you can trust me." We didn't talk on the ride home. Three turns, and I was at my front door. I waved goodbye and stepped inside. I kicked off my shoes, locked the door and stripped before climbing into bed.

* * *

My phone was ringing. I ignored it, but it rang again and again. Finally, I crawled out of bed and dug for it in my purse. It was Ashland. *What time is it?* I saw that it was 8 a.m. I was exhausted; wasn't he?

I yawned and answered the phone. "Hey! Good morning. You're up awful early..."

"Come to the house. I'm sorry to wake you up, but I need you to come over." The urgency in his voice was palpable.

"What is it? Is everything okay?" I stood, my body tense. Did they vandalize the place? What mischief was Mia into now?

"TD called me this morning. He found Matthews. He's dead, Carrie Jo."

I sat on the edge of the bed, barely able to process what I had just heard. "What? How did he...I mean, when did he..."

"I don't know anything. But because of the report we made, the police want to talk to everyone who was there last night."

"Of course. I'll be there in fifteen minutes."

"Thanks, Carrie Jo." He hung up, and I scrambled to get dressed. I couldn't believe this was happening.

Since I began working at Seven Sisters, I've lost my best friend, who appears to have some serious unexplained issues with me. I've lost a sort-of boyfriend but found a guy I really like. I've met several "ghosts" and have had a lapful of mysteries thrown my way. Am I now going to be a murder suspect?

I didn't know what to think about all of it, but there was one thing I did know. Seven Sisters was a place where life and death happened, where fear and hope resided—a place where things were lost and things were found.

I wondered what today was going to bring...

Read on for Chapter 1 of

Moonlights Falls at Seven Sisters…

I swung my Honda into the long driveway that led to the antebellum home, doing my best to navigate the maze of police cars and emergency vehicles. It was an odd sight: the swirling red and blue lights cast against the fading white columns and the green-gray mold that covered the chipping paint, evidence of many wet, humid Alabama seasons gone by. It was just a little after 7 a.m., and it had been a long night with too little sleep.

Ashland met me at the car. His drawn face and clenched square jaw were evidence that he was angry and disturbed. Hollis Matthews, the attorney who had hired me had been found dead, apparently murdered, somewhere in the building. "Hey, thanks for coming over so fast. Listen, the police want to talk to us about last night, but don't go in yet. They are about to take him out."

I stepped out of the car, suddenly aware of how wild my wavy, long hair must look. I gathered it up in a ponytail holder. I searched his blue eyes, "Are you okay?" I had not been a fan of the fastidious attorney, and I wasn't sure how close he and Ashland had been, but it was upsetting no matter what.

"I'll be fine." He led me by the elbow to a police car. "This is Detective Simmons. She will be investigating the... she's in charge of the investigation." Detective Simmons looked to be in her late 40s, with bright red hair and a freckled complexion. She was tall and pale, and she looked like she knew what she was doing.

I put my hand out. "Hello, Detective. I am Carrie Jo Jardine. I'm part of the research team here."

"Thanks for coming, Ms. Jardine." After a quick handshake, she got down to business. "What is your connection with the folks that were here last night? I understand that the woman," she consulted her notebook, "Mia Reed, worked with you here? How long have you known her?"

"Um....yes, we went to school together. I can't believe Mia would be involved with this, but...then again, I've discovered recently that I don't really know her like I thought I did."

"What do you mean by that, Miss Jardine?" The detective shielded her pale green eyes from the sun that was rising, along with the heat.

I thought about the conversation I heard yesterday through the cast-iron floor gates. It was Mia and Matthews, plotting about something, something that I was pretty sure concerned me. Was I sure it was Mia? I decided against sharing what I heard. I didn't hear everything, and Ashland was standing next to me. I didn't want to look like a backstabbing friend, even though I wasn't. "Well, when we caught her up here with her friends, she tried to say that I gave her permission to be here, but I never did. I think they were having a séance—or something. I would never have agreed to that."

"You say she was having a séance? Who were these other people?" Detective Simmons pursed her dark red lips as she waited for my answer.

"I don't know exactly what they were doing. There was a lot of chanting, and it was just plain strange. The other people were Henri Devecheaux, a local guy. He gave me his card." I felt my pockets, but the card wasn't in these jeans. "It's at my apartment. I can call you with the information later. The other guy was William, William Bettencourt. He was a mutual friend of ours from Charleston." I hadn't yet told Ashland that William had been my sort-of boyfriend, and this was certainly not the right time to share.

The medical examiners were caring out Matthews' covered body. As they passed us, I shivered and looked away, at the ground, at the sky, anywhere else. I had never seen a dead body before, at least not in my real life.

"Let's go inside and get out of the sun," Ashland offered. I followed him, and the detective walked behind me, but I was nervous about going in. I didn't know how he had died and where. I didn't want to be disrespectful.

From the way that police were moving up and down the hall, I could tell that whatever had taken place here had been in the Blue Room. Many tragic events had played out there, against a timeless backdrop of beauty and perceived elegance. In the current restoration project, the Blue Room was ground zero for our operations. It was our computer center, where my team and I worked to produce layouts for each of the rooms and gather the antiques and supplies needed to set them up as a living museum in honor of Old Mobile. It was my temporary workplace; when we completed the project, our work area would be moved off-site, but this was how Matthews had wanted it. He wanted us to work here, in the house. I didn't know why, but I was happy to oblige—this was a once-in-a-lifetime gig. Now the gray-haired lawyer with the cold gray eyes was as dead as those buried in the mausoleum just a few hundred yards away.

"Can you tell me if anything is missing from the house? I mean, I know it's a big one and you've got a lot of boxes here, but could you and Mr. Stuart look around and tell me if anything is gone?" I nodded, and Ashland I walked around, careful not to touch anything. I was happy to note that whatever fear had struck me last night, whatever creepy apparition I had believed I had heard, was gone now. The warmth of the day and the cheery sunshine had pushed the shadows away, taming them back to the darkness where they belonged. We strolled through the downstairs, except the Blue Room, and didn't notice anything out of place. The detective followed us around as we did our inventory. The mantelpieces were there. The paintings from the LeMans family, very expensive paintings of antebellum pets were still leaning against the wall, wrapped in paper. They had been Mia's find.

Finally, we climbed up the wooden spiral staircase, and I followed Ashland as we toured each room. The first room had once been the guest room, and all was in order. We traveled through each room with nothing to report. The door to Calpurnia's room was standing open, and the chalk markings were still on the floor, evidence of Mia's amateur séance. I shivered again, remembering the anguished cries of *Mon dieu!*, and Ashland put his hand on my shoulder.

"Nope, nothing missing here either. The only room left is the Blue Room. Is it possible for us to go in there, or should we wait?" I could hear the strain in his voice. For the first time, I noticed that he hadn't changed since the night before. He looked crumpled and tired.

"Sure, let's go see if they're finished." Detective Simmons walked down the staircase ahead of us. I grabbed Ashland's hand. "Do you want me to go in? I mean, you don't have to right now."

He gave me his best college football star smile. "No, I'll be okay. I know he wasn't a friendly guy, but he helped me through some rough times. I need to see what happened. Let's go." We headed to the Blue Room, now empty of emergency workers, except for a few stragglers talking quietly in a corner near the printer.

Immediately, my eyes were drawn to my desk. The music box was gone! The one that Rachel Kowalski had handed me yesterday. I had set it on my desk when I came downstairs. Now it was gone.

"The music box is gone." I walked to my desk and looked underneath it. "Can I pull out the drawers?"

Detective Simmons looked at one of the other officers.

"Yeah, we're done in here." The pair left us with the detective. I opened the drawers on the off chance that I had stuffed the box inside one, but they were all empty.

"What did it look like?" Ashland asked.

"It was about eight inches long, maybe five inches wide, rectangular. It had an ornate domed lid, probably made from ivory with enamel and wood inlays. There was a dancing lady on the top—Rachel brought it to me yesterday. I set it here." Puzzled, I stood up and tapped my desk. I looked again and again, and it was certainly gone.

"Was this item valuable?" Detective Simmons stood across from the desk from me. "Maybe valuable enough to kill someone over?"

"It's valuable in the sense that it has historical value; it is an antebellum music box that actually works, which makes it rare. But as far as killing someone for it... I don't see that happening. I mean, look around. If you were here to rob the place, wouldn't you take a computer or some of other equipment? You know, equipment that you could pawn or sell to someone? What are they going to do with a music box?"

The detective gave me a crooked smile. "That's the question, isn't it? Listen, do you have a picture of this box you could send me?"

"No, I hadn't photographed it yet. It wasn't really a part of any of the exhibits. I guess I could find a photo of something similar to show you. Might take a while, though."

"That's fine. We've got plenty to work on here. I guess that's it for now, then. You plan on staying in Mobile, or are you going back to Charleston?"

"I don't have any plans to leave, Detective."

She flipped her book closed. "Good. That makes my job so much easier. Mr. Stuart, I will be in touch." With a curt nod, she left Ashland and me alone.

Except for a few spots of blood on the carpet, there was no sign of a struggle or even a crime. Ashland sat in Mia's old chair, leaning his elbows on his knees and holding his head. "I can't believe this. Who would want to kill him? And why would they do it here?"

I pulled up a chair close to him and put my hand on his arm. "Does he have any family? Someone we should call?"

"I've got my office taking care of that. He had a sister, I think, but he never talked about her. I don't even know her name. He said she was sick, and that was it. I guess I'm the only family he had besides her. I know he was distant, but he believed in this restoration as much as I did. As a matter of fact, it was Matthews that pushed me towards completing my family's legacy. If it weren't for him, I don't think I would have even started this. But now that it has begun, I have to see it through. I couldn't help my mother, but I can restore this place for her, and for my family, for the people who lived here—and died here." He added the last with raw sadness.

"Listen, do you want to take some time off the project, at least until after the funeral?" I wanted to help him but I wasn't sure how yet. This was a way to start.

He gave me a weak smile. "No, we are going to stay on schedule. That's what he would have wanted." He put his arm around me and hugged me. I hugged him back. He stood up, and we began walking to the door. "Going forward, I'm going to need more of your help with things around here. I am counting on you to bring Seven Sisters back to life."

"I'm here, Ashland. I'm not going anywhere." I could see the tears in his eyes. I pulled him close and kissed him. We stood together at the foot of the stairs, our arms around each other. From upstairs, I could hear movement, and then it stopped. Ashland didn't seem to notice, but as we stepped apart and turned to leave, I heard a soft sigh.

It was probably just the house, the wood expanding from the heat of the day, the metal shifting along the porch railing. Maybe it was a draft, blowing through some silk curtains.

Whatever it was, I wasn't afraid. I had Ashland by my side.

Read more from M.L. Bullock

The Seven Sisters Series

Seven Sisters
Moonlight Falls on Seven Sisters
Shadows Stir at Seven Sisters
The Stars that Fell
The Stars We Walked Upon
The Sun Rises Over Seven Sisters (forthcoming)

The Desert Queen Series

The Tale of Nefret
The Falcon Rises
The Kingdom of Nefertiti
The Song of the Bee-Eater (forthcoming)

The Sugar Hill Series (forthcoming)

Wife of the Left Hand
The Ramparts
Blood By Candlelight

The Sirens Gate Series (forthcoming)

The Mermaid's Gift
The Blood Feud
The Wrath of Minerva
The Lorelei Curse
The Fortunate Star

The Southern Gothic Series

Being with Beau

To receive updates on her latest releases,
visit her website at MLBullock.com
and subscribe to her mailing list.